Permanent for Now

a novel

Permanent for Now

a novel

Jeffrey S. Markovitz

Permanent for Now
Copyright © 2018 by Jeffrey S. Markovitz.
All Rights Reserved
Published by Unsolicited Press
Printed in the United States of America.
First Edition: December 2018

Attention schools and businesses: for discounted copies on large orders, please contact the publisher directly.

This book is a work of fiction. Names, characters, businesses, organizations, places, events and incidents either are the product of the author's imagination or are used fictitiously. Any resemblance to actual persons, living or dead, events, or locales is entirely coincidental.

For information contact:
Unsolicited Press
Portland, Oregon
www.unsolicitedpress.com
orders@unsolicitedpress.com
619-354-8005

Book and Cover design by Kelly McQuain
Editor: Olivia Cyr
Editor: Taylor Scheubel

ISBN: 978-1-947021-73-0

10 9 8 7 6 5 4 3 2 1

CONTENTS

"Each of us has Heaven and Hell in him."
—Oscar Wilde

"I make the poem of evil also, I
commemorate that part
    also,
I am myself just as much evil as good,
and my nation is — and
   I say there is in fact no evil,
(Or if there is I say it is just as important
to you, to the land or to
    me, as any thing else.)"
—Walt Whitman

*(What difference is there between love and
loss? A fricative taken away, two sibilants
added.*

*I have lost it forever, my lovely v.
I got in exchange the cruelest sound.)*
—Edmond Jabés

Elbflorenz

Chapter 1

He died.

Chapter 2

The water pressure is low and the walls are thin so I can hear the cocks crowing a block away at the Vietnamese butchery. Though it is morning, it is not yet dawn. The cocks project their penetrating voices all day, as if, on display, are cleavers destined for their necks, swinging pendulums from nails; they shout their pious pleas for freedom through the bars of their world and out into the sky.

I wash my bald knuckles, the hairs seared and curled upon themselves after being scorched by the burners on my stove. I wash my bald head, my fragile body. It moves slowly, my body, to wash itself. I am careful of slipping; the lather circles, a buzzard over the partly clogged drain, and lubricates the floor of the stall. If I slip, it could be the last thing I do. The first thing Lombard South said to me was "You're a survivor." And he said it with such excitement that for a moment, I felt it, too. Excitement. Now, all I smell is my burnt knuckle hair and all I hear are cocks and all I am is fragile.

I breathe.

For this, I am grateful and I am ashamed.

My alarm clock this morning was set at six because it was set at six the day before. It will be set at six tomorrow. Every morning, I watch it until it goes off, never leaving the bed until it does, until it calls me to my feet. I lie there, regardless of when I wake up, and watch the analogue hands spin until they are spread at their furthest distance, their most impossible clap, and a bell tells me to rise. I am used to commands. It sometimes takes me a half hour, rising. I remember being a boy, alive at the pistol shot of a cock's crow, up and out and everywhere. There wasn't enough in the world for me to ignore any part of it, so I woke up running. This many years later, I open my eyes and think, again, *my body has shrunk*. It is leaving me, this body, day after day, until it will be gone and I will be without it. I think of myself separate from it. There is a body of a man, old and fragile and shrinking. And there is me, inside, trapped, a cock in a cage, howling silently to be a boy intrigued enough by the world to remain ignorant of it.

This morning, as every other, I could not squeeze the cold from my fingers, so I held them hovering above the burner while staring at the blank wall behind the stove. I remembered to forget, but loud sounds in my memory caused me to take quick inward breaths in succession. All ins and no outs. Small and forceful, like sniffs of fractionally fragrant flowers, but through the mouth—filling my lungs until they might have burst. Loud sounds in memory. And I exhaled, breathed in through my nose, and then smelled the singe of knuckle hair that hovered with my hands, a little too close to the flame.

All bodies are ultimately frail.

It has taken a while, a slow, careful, considerate time, but I am clean. For a moment, I let the water slap at me. I hold the Brillo pad against the stream of water, allowing it to spray in chaotic directions. The metal wires reflect the peach light from the bathroom's solitary bulb, dimmed by dead flies in the fixture, and I bring it to my arm.

They are not mine. The numbers. I don't want them.

Lombard South said to me, without provocation, without introduction, "You're a survivor." And his excitement was contagious, but only momentarily. I didn't know what he meant at first, by calling me that. He just said it. So I looked at him like *he* was the crazy man, like *he* was the old man carrying a grocery bag of only a few things, because any more and the weight would be too much to bear on the walk home. Like *he* was the one who should have worn a long-sleeved shirt that day, as he should have every day. Catching my confusion, South nodded his forehead at my left arm. Between the wrist and the elbow, grey for the world to see: numbers. And I turned them from him, the numbers that aren't mine, pulling my arm from his view, and I shook my head, "I've survived nothing."

I work the Brillo pad back and forth slowly at first, until the friction numbs the surface of my skin. One thing I've learned, one truth, is that after a specific amount of pain, you begin to feel nothing. After the initial shock, there's just nothing there. So when I feel nothing, at the exact moment when there's nothing there, I push hard and rub quickly, scratching and digging deep. I try to take away what were never mine. Numbers. A gift unasked for.

Tiny dribbles of blood find the shower floor and disperse, rose-pink to clear, gone with the water.

I stop, and they're there. Raw skin above, but sunk still and shadowy.

They will always be there. Grey signals of survival.

Though I've survived nothing.

I turn off the shower and hope I do not slip getting out. Remarkably, I still want to cling to life.

This is what I want for myself when I die: my body cremated, and portions of my feathery ash distributed to my dearest dear friends, so that they can disperse me alone and in secret, at the places they remember us most fondly. Golden urns clasped in the shaking hands of my closest companions, who, after eulogy and tears, rub me into the ground at their feet at the place we met, or the place we enjoyed, or the place we said goodbye. I want to be all over the world, the way I woke up dreaming to be as a boy.

What is true is that I do not have those dearest dear friends, so my ashes will flutter as feathers dropped from birds unexpectedly freed to unmarked ground, harboring no memories of me.

CHAPTER 3

In Dresden, everyone was whispering.

No one could wrap themselves tightly enough in their coats to force away the cold, but they squeezed anyway, pushing the edges of cloth into each other around their bodies. Tight like Christmas presents wrapped hastily because of excitement, with little tears at the corners, because of excitement. The cold snaked its way into the coats of the people of Dresden, biting the places on the bodies it found. Men with hunched backs and drawn up shoulders stood on the corners with their caps pulled down over their foreheads and whispered. When someone passed, they'd lower their voices, as if the Allies could hear, and perhaps coughed into a balled fist. They were suspicious, but mostly, they were afraid.

Bridget Erinnerung held a small burlap sack with a few small potatoes above her pregnant belly as she ambled through Altmarkt. She channeled all of her warmth into her womb. Her path was through the square where stones were placed at such strange intervals that there were uneven gaps between them. She was mindful of each foot's placement as they tempted steps against the chasms. The winter of 1919 was the coldest she could ever remember, yet the people of the city still filled Altmarkt as if it were spring. There was a quiet commotion.

Something was happening. It was apparent in the nothing happening.

But Bridget did not have time to ponder the whispering men, the strange, guarded postures of people in cafés. The way people moved around quickly as if they sensed someone was behind them, the untrusting examination of one another. She did not care to stop and inquire what it was that brought so many people out into the open on that cold day. She had two children at home, one inside of her, and a husband dead from the war.

A boy ran by her at great speed, a plaid felt hat flapping in his hand with the disturbance of wind around him. She watched him glide by and turn his head, looking over his shoulder to say, "Sorry, Miss."

"You'd think he'd be on fire how he's running to the river," said the voice of a man nearby.

Bridget turned toward the voice and nodded at Ernst Klein, the dairy man, who stood with his stomach hanging over his belt and his fingernails scratching his scalp in a non-contemplative way. Milk bottles sat steadily in a satchel attached to his waistband. He looked at her pleasantly but there was an aberration of untruth to the look, as if there was nothing pleasant in his head prompting the corresponding look from his face.

"I'm only afraid he'll fall," Bridget said.

"Then he falls. Boys fall."

Bridget assumed it was so, but she thought of Gregor, her eldest, and couldn't nod her agreement. She turned around again and watched the boy run around the Frauenkirche and out of sight. Though the streets were uncannily full, they were the same old streets they always were. A constant. A regular. They curved to the right and swept to the left, creating the winding enigma that smelled and felt of old place. Dresden was old, full of old. Full of places where other people walked; ancient people, as real and regal as mythology. Forefathers in antique hats and coats. People walked Dresden's arteries hundreds of years before any distant past Bridget could presume to conceive. It was an old feeling, but not an elderly one. It did not feel weak, tired. Dresden felt young and open and alive.

When she was carrying Gregor, she couldn't believe that something lived inside of her, depended on her. She felt like a girl still; she *was* a girl. And suddenly, she was this other thing. A mother. A name with so much connotation. Bridget likened being a mother to owning something precious, like being the bearer of a priceless porcelain egg that teetered precariously from a precipice ledge, for which she was the woman below holding a pillow. However, when Gregor was born, when he tried to open his eyes for the first time and found light simply too much, she knew he was no precious egg, he was a human being. Hatched. And in that, there was something much more that she'd need to be. Much more than a woman with a pillow.

It made her sicker to her stomach than the pregnancy nausea.

Bridget looked at the gaps between the stones and remembered what Ernst had just said. *Boys fall.* "Not to say that they should, though," she said.

"A scraped knee is a pace slower tomorrow. I've spent my time amongst these stones."

"Yes."

Ernst looked at Bridget's pregnant belly without coyness or delicacy. He knew her situation too well. No woman in her condition would ever be carrying potatoes home in this absolute cold, unless. Well, he thought to himself, unless she had to. When Bridget breathed out, her breath was thick and visible. A wind came by and took it away to the clouds.

Her stomach bubbled audibly.

Between the two was a chasm of everything left unsaid.

"There's nothing here," she said.

"Miss?"

"What will they do to us?"

He thought. He answered too quickly, "What they have to."

Bridget couldn't help but look at the milk on Ernst's belt. He followed her eyes. Pulling a small carafe from its holster and an empty one from another, Ernst proceeded to fill the empty one halfway.

"Please," he said, stretching out his arm with the half carafe bottle of milk in his hand.

"No," replied Bridget, still staring at cracks, "I will not be forced to be wild."

Ernst looked at her. If she was truly offended, she would have gone. "If the baby is to get your milk, you will need milk yourself."

The child inside of her had grown into a boy in nine quick months. Gregor seemed to wait forever to appear. Adette, her second child, took her time as well. But this child, this person, grew so fast inside of her, it was as if he couldn't wait to join the world, a world Bridget felt apprehensive introducing him to. A world that took his father, and would most surely ask of him things he would be forced to do for reasons not his own. Bridget pictured this boy without a face (she could not yet picture what she had not yet seen), as a soldier on a barren winter field with the sun pulled far away from the Earth, a rifle nudged snugly between his shoulder and his neck, warm from firing. Perhaps this boy would have to make up an excuse in the harsh winters ahead to fire his gun in order to use the nozzle to warm his neck. Who would have to consume the bullet for his warmth?

But she was not allowed to think that way of an unborn baby. She knew, no matter what they became, and no matter why, a baby had to be cared for. A baby had to have its milk, regardless.

So Bridget placed the carafe into her potato sack and left Ernst Klein on the busy old street.

A few blocks from home, Bridget knelt down. She clutched her stomach and pulled back her lips in an agony that looked like a smile. Inside of her, the boy was restless; it was time. The potatoes rolled from her sack onto the ground and the carafe of milk plummeted and broke against the mismatched cobbles. The liquid ran through the small gaps between the laid stones like white Venetian canals; Bridget closed her eyes and imagined gondolas. She thought of her husband, lying back carelessly in one, with her in a summer dress in the opposite end. It was their fantasy to see Italy. The sort of fantasy they used, in their youthful courting, to hold reality at an impasse. It was a trench dug around their plateau of young hope that showed itself in a smile between them when older generations would regard the couple with the smug contemplation of seasoned marriages. As Bridget now pictured it, there was no gondolier, and that subtle fact (along with the more obvious and treacherous fact) made her fantasy a fantasy only.

When she opened her eyes, she thought there would be men in warm coats bending down around her to help her rise. There were none. They were in the cafés, whispering. They were in the square, hunching their shoulders and worrying about what would become of them and their neighbors, while one such neighbor had just gone into labor.

Gregor ran down the street with haste; she saw him coming. She wished he had a felt hat, no direction, and a wild mischievous smile attached to an apologetic voice as he terrorized people in the square with his playful jaunt; instead, he was hurrying frightened to his fallen mother. His shoes were falling apart, but he was quick and responsible. His strides were little hops, gazelle-like, and quick, accelerated by the fear that something bad had happened to her. Gregor was a good boy, she knew, so much like his father. Frightened like his father, who joined the war because every man joined the war. Bridget never thought of her doomed husband as joining the army; he was joining the *war*. Without so much as understanding a portion of the politics behind the conflict—Bridget did not think of nationality, nor of land acquisition—she recognized that he was becoming part of something larger than an army. She knew that people who joined a war never separated from it, even if they survived. War, you became. The things you do in war become you, regardless of your duty, your fault, or which army's insignia you bear. When Gregor's father left to join the war, Bridget said goodbye, not to him, but to the part of him that would never come back.

He never did come back. Not even as a facsimile.

He left her a son as a gift to remember him by.

A daughter too timid.

And another someone inside of her.

"I was looking out of the window," Gregor said, as he approached her. His momentum was so fast that she feared he would barrel into her. He slowed just in time and went down to his knees. "I was looking out of the window." And he was, the whole time she was gone. While Adette shivered in the corner, Gregor was at the window, waiting for his mother and the potatoes. And though it didn't occur to him, he waited also for his brother.

Gregor helped his mother to her feet and they walked down the street. At six, Gregor couldn't hold her hand in any way that would support her, so he pushed her from behind, putting all of his weight in careful forward momentum toward the door of their home. Bridget stopped at the end of the first block, against the force of his insistence, turned to him, and said, "Get the potatoes."

"Mother?"

"Get the potatoes."

He looked at her, scared to separate from the only person in the world who came home to him. Even abstractly, he knew the world to be so large, and she was all he had to not be lost in it and alone. A six-year-old boy, drowning in the size of the ocean.

"Get the potatoes," Bridget repeated a final time, "and be careful of the glass."

The midwife put something cold and lubricated in the palm of her left hand and rubbed it violently with her right. "You're lucky your boy came and got me, you're very close."

Bridget did not comment, she just looked over at Gregor and considered his speed. He held Adette in the corner of their small apartment. It was on the highest level of their building, accessible only by stairs, and in her last trimester, it took Bridget the better part of a half hour to climb them to her door. While Gregor ran for the midwife, it took Bridget only forty-five minutes to ascend. Their home was one room with a solitary window that looked out with a wonderful vantage over Altstadt. The view was the family's greatest source of entertainment, as Bridget would point to each building and name it for her children. She would tell them how old each structure was. That church, she'd say, is so old, that the people who built it had to carry the stones on their backs. No, Gregor would say. Yes. One by one.

The children would muse at the buildings with the sort of reverence they deserved. Ancient relics from another time, proving, at least, that there were people before them, and proving, to an extent, that there would be people after. "Do you see that?" she once asked Gregor.

"The Frauenkirche?"

"Yes Gregor, the Frauenkirche. That is there for you." It was the church they attended every Sunday, to pray and listen to the organ and stare at the dome that seemed to rise straight up to Heaven itself.

"For me?"

"Yes. It was built for you. To always run around it. And it will always be there, no matter what. If you're ever frightened, I want you to run around it. Around and around." On Sundays, the organ filled the dome with tonal smoke. From the window, the building seemed different to Gregor, as if it were impossible that something so far away could also be something that he entered each week. On the inside, it was a loud spectacle that made him squint at the murals in the nave; from their apartment window, it was an untouchable relic, a beauty his mother insisted was his, but that he felt uneasy touching, because it somehow represented her.

Gregor studied it with vivacity. Each finely crafted edge, the mighty rising cupola and its arches, through which Gregor could see sky.

Aside from their one window, there was a stove and sink along one wall, where the midwife would often direct Gregor for a fresh bowl of water. There was a small cabinet, a bed, and nothing more. The family slept in the one room, not comfortably, but together.

Bridget's agitation rose as the baby began to make its move. She knew the pain, remembered it immediately. It was remote at first, as was her memory of it, a feeling she had felt only twice before in her life. But it came fast, and with it, her ability to manage the apartment ceded to little Gregor, who calmed his little sister by telling her their mother was okay, that she acted the same way when little Adette was born, though that was a lie. Gregor was not present when Adette was born.

The midwife whispered, "Peace." Bridget's response was only partial and consisted of no comprehensible word. "Peace," the midwife repeated. "They're considering calling it a 'Treaty of Peace.'" Bridget quickly understood why she was whispering. It was the same reason everyone in Dresden was whispering. The same fear that existed in the visible breath between two men at a café's door, between men standing on the corner; the same fear that shook Ernst's hand when he gave Bridget the milk. The same fear that seemed to widen the stones in the square, creating larger gaps of peril. The same fear that made the midwife forget her duties.

"Please," Bridget muttered.

"Peace," the midwife responded, "so much peace we won't eat."

And Bridget fainted.

When she awoke, the midwife said, "We push now." Bridget closed her weary eyes and in the dark that resulted, a gondola, soothingly empty, floated by.

In Paris, men sat around and talked about how to reconstruct the world, while in Dresden, Mirko Erinnerung was born.

CHAPTER 4

The memorial is bronze with twisted human bodies intertwined to make a flame.

Lombard South stands behind me as if supporting me; he thinks I may fall. But I know I won't. Not here or now. I am to be strong.

I whisper, "Now I must face my history," and South is quiet-reverent as if he were in a church. Or a graveyard. The sky is that perfect, open, beautiful sky that happens only a few times a year. This sort of sky we saw at the camp, a perfect contradiction to the land it hovered above. I can almost look up and imagine I am there.

I am always there.

South is patient. I don't walk very fast to begin with and he is courteous the way you'd hope a person would be careful with an old man visiting a memorial for something in his very own memory. He helps me walk around it, the human flame, and I see all of the intricacies of the sculptor's work: the faces, the hands reaching.

South says, "Small stones," and I point at a few loose stones on the ground and point next at the cylindrical platform the flame is affixed to, where there is a fortune of small, rounded stones gathered. They are placed purposefully. He understands. South picks up a stone from the ground and places it with the others on the platform. Then, he repeats the gesture for me.

Then what we do is breathe in and breathe out. We do this because we are alive.

I get the feeling that South wants people to see the numbers on my arm, to know that I've come to this place to connect with a part of my past. But this is unfair to him; for me to presume to know what he wants is foolish. Perhaps it is me who wants to parade myself.

After the Liberation, I came to America with many others; we all thought of America as the freest place on Earth. The contrast of supreme captivity to supreme freedom was too much for some of us, who had the decision of where we wanted to go, to ignore. Most were not lucky enough to choose their destination. Though freed, the majority of diaspora still went where they were taken. No longer captive, we were captivated with the thought of returning home, but the riptide that was the war's end left our homes smoldering gorges in the Earth, so we laid back and let the ocean carry us to the other side of the world.

Washington D.C. is different now, in 2002—the palindrome number that is this year. I cannot believe that I am alive to see it. On newspapers, it shocks me every time. 2002. The year in which I am now alive. If you were to ask me what year I would live to see back then, I would say, *this year*. *This* is the year I will see. Not 2002, but the year that was present then. The year that was permanent. But one year relinquished itself to another, dominoes tipped, and I've gotten here. I've woken up, one day at a time, as I've taken one step at a time, and *that* life has become *this* life will become the next life, and so on. D.C. has changed, as with all things, but some of it is the same.

For the first twenty years, I found myself sitting outside of small cafés watching dogs and allowing my hair to silver. I would smoke cigarettes and they would invigorate my lungs. I'd sit close to the curb at the outdoor tables, breathing in exhaust as cars paused at stop signs. The mixture of exhaust and nicotine filled the folds in my lungs, poisons I breathed gladly. The dogs would watch me back, as interested in me as I was them. Their curious lives brought so much comfort to me while I sat at those cafés, though I never owned a dog myself. I just couldn't. A life dependent on me would be too subtle an irony. And when the owner of a dog would look over at me watching his dog,

I would turn away, look into my cooled coffee or crumbs of cake. The dogs always looked sad but never were.

The following years made my silver hair fall out.

I wore a long-sleeved shirt almost every day, even in summer.

I made enough money to stay alive, which is what I did.

When I first met Lombard South, he said, "You're a survivor." But what he really said was, "Oh my God, you're a survivor."

I had to rest once every block from the outdoor market to my front door. If there was a bench, I would sit on it, lowering the plastic bag of groceries next to me and trying to catch my breath, elusive as it was. If there wasn't a bench, I would sit on the curb. D.C. was a wealth of outdoor markets, and when I first arrived in the city, one such market was the first place I found myself. I had a brown hat and a suitcase with nothing in it, save for one small slip of paper with an address and an allowance of money. But I had no idea how to locate the building that would house me for the next many decades of my life; the slip of paper had letters and numbers and words that I found out were state names, compass point indicators, and streets or avenues. It seemed code, and I gave up perhaps too quickly. I noticed people where a street was closed to traffic and walked with my hat and empty suitcase over to them. I hadn't seen an outdoor market since my childhood. So I walked around and bought an apple with the change I had been given. Every week, from then on, I would walk the little way from the apartment, which I eventually found, to and from the market with the food I'd purchased.

I had never seen South before he pulled back the door to my building and held it for me. I would learn that he had just moved from Philadelphia the week before. It had taken me the better part of an hour to walk home from the market that day, and my small bag of groceries was the most my feeble arms could carry home. It was no matter, I was eating less and less. Shrinking. It felt almost good to suffer.

South had noticed my numbers and said what he said. I always wore a long-sleeved shirt, my closet full of sleeves, but that day I didn't, foolishly. He was a thick man, bald but lean and very fit. South seemed in his late thirties. He commanded the space around him, something about his composure suggesting that he was used to order, that perhaps he was used to maintaining it. Because of this, instantly, I was afraid of him. He tried to smile, but his muscles had defined ridges and his jaw was sharp with the skin pulled taut around it. He'd clench his teeth and pulse out a bone beneath each ear. The most unsettling part, however, was that he looked straight into my eyes. This was something that I never did. It is something that I never do. He looked me straight in the eyes and did not avert at awkward silence. He did not gaze at the ground or thumb the loops of his jeans contemplatively. He just looked into my eyes like he was watching a movie. And he waited for me to enter the apartment, which I did not. He reached out his hand and said, "Lombard South" but I did not understand him. I also did not take his hand. I had never heard an accent like his before. It was thick like him, muddled and spoken quickly with many syllables in abstention. He changed the sounds of vowels. His vocabulary was uncommon everywhere except for where he was from. With his hand untook, he made a move to grab my bag of groceries. I was not quick enough to withdraw, so South had my food and was moving up the stairs in front of me, looking through the bag, asking which apartment was mine, telling me he had just moved from Philadelphia, and exclaiming that I seemed to live on a "shit diet."

I told myself to follow him quickly, but my body responded by following him slowly.

When I got to my apartment, he was there on the landing, somehow omniscient in knowing which was my door. Because I could do nothing else, I inserted and turned the key, and let him in. I still had not said a word.

South put my groceries on the counter and said, "Welp, nice to meet you, eh. . ."

It was an invitation to tell him my name. I hesitated, said nothing.

"Okay. Well hey," South said, moving to my door in a couple quick strides, "maybe we can sit, talk, you know. I'd like to maybe talk a little about all of that shit, the Holocaust and everything."

I nodded accidently. It seemed there was nothing he wasn't comfortable with.

"Good," he said. "Have a good one," and left my apartment.

And that's how it got to be that he would come to my apartment here and again, with all the free time he had in the world, to talk about the Holocaust and everything.

I don't say much, but it doesn't seem to bother South, ever. We take laps around the monument here in Baltimore. South drove north. He offered. Told me there were memorials in every city.

I said, "What memorials?"

"You know."

"No."

"For like the Jews and all."

Yes, the Jews. And all.

And he offered to drive me up to Baltimore to see one. What is true is that I am too weak to reject an idea, and South is the sort of persistent that doesn't wait for confirmations to his suggestions. This was about a year after he first held the door open for me.

We're right downtown, and it is the middle of the day, so cars drive down the block, stop for traffic lights, then continue on. Two men sit on the corner and watch our every move. Between them are open-ended, light-brown paper bags weighted to the sidewalk. The bags are crumpled at the neck, fresh from grabbing, and I watch them with my eyes pushed to the extreme side of their sockets, all periphery, as if I don't want them to know I'm looking. I hear South mutter "Bums" but I don't respond. Instead, I try to read the writing on the memorial, but can't. I squint.

When South knocked on my door after our first encounter with the groceries, I didn't answer it. I pretended that I was out by staying very still, which is a skill bestowed upon the old. I knew, eventually, South would knock and I would have to answer the door; if he knocked enough times without an answer, he'd become concerned and the next thing I'd know, firemen would be axing through my apartment door. Since I had come to America, I made no close friends. In a way, I found it very difficult to want to relate to others, to want to speak with them. Invariably, there would be situations over the long years where I would cross paths with potential friends, perhaps even lovers, but I would quell the fire until it quit before it had its hot hooks in me. That is not to say that I was content. Quite the opposite. I was very lonely; I wanted more than anything to talk with someone, to tell someone what happened to me. But I could not. Biologically, I could not. There was a steel trap in my throat locked with the padlock of my tongue.

This is because I am a coward.

And I became an old man, as men do.

South knocked on my door again, and when I answered that next time, he said hello and waved a six pack of beer back and forth in front of my face, as if to hypnotize me. I turned around and walked back into the apartment as a means of welcome, and he followed, eager to dispel all the pleasantries he learned over the years.

"What a dump, brother."

I kept walking slowly to the couch.

"I'm just fuckin' with you. Anyway, you want a beer, yeah?"

I did not answer him, so he unscrewed the top from one and placed it on the coffee table in front of me. Throughout that visit, I learned a lot about Lombard South but he didn't learn anything about me. He drank five beers and got very sleepy. When he made to go, he said, "Thanks for the chat," and rose, brushing off imaginary dust from the front of his shirt and breathing out so loud that his breath sounded *huuhhhhh*. His arms made a strong sweeping motion down across his torso, and when he walked to the door, I tried to get up, but stayed right where I was. From the door, he called, "See you later," and shut it.

I had not said a word. The beer in front of me was warm. But for the first time in a very long time, I didn't feel alone.

"Crazy shit, yeah?"

I nod. There's not much more to this memorial than the flame of people, though I'm not sure what else there needs to be. South pats me on the back and says, "I'm hungry." I don't laugh but I want to. Some people would say *how can you be hungry at a place like this?* But I agree, I'm hungry too.

In that way, of South coming to my apartment and drinking five beers while I watched one warm, we became a sort of friends. I did not know what he wanted from me, but I welcomed him the only way I could, by turning from the door and allowing him to enter. And of course, time went on, because that's what it loves to do, and I warmed enough to South to say something here and again. He never acted shocked. Never said, "Well well well, look who's talking now!" He just responded to whatever I said like any decent person would respond, the way they're supposed to. And South never asked me about my grey numbers, nor did he ask me to tell him my story, not directly. He would mention things implicitly to spur me into conversation, dangle a hook in front of my face with savory temptations, but I was never biting.

He'd say, "Did you see on the History Channel?"

And, "There's a genocide going on in Africa right now, yeah?"

Then there was the time when he blew out a candle between us, and while the dead smoke of the flame rose slowly into our field of vision, he told me there were memorials in every city and that, yeah?, we should go on road trips and see them.

What I wanted was to say *no*. What South said was, "Yes, that's what we'll do."

Part of me thinks that South is the most careful and sensitive man, the way he wanted to bring me here so I could connect with the past. That's what he told me, at least. Though I've never said in so many words that it was something I needed to do, connect. Some severances are good and purposeful. And it isn't to get a reaction. I am not the end of an experiment for him, to see what would happen if put face to face with a personal tragedy. Why South took it upon himself to drive me here, to come to my apartment time after time to talk to me, is because *he* needs it. Like in all cases, South's motivations are self-propelled; he needs to feel he is helping me because he needs help himself.

Though, of course, this is just me pretending to know what someone else needs.

What I do know is that he is hungry. Like myself. People who need to eat.

Chapter 5

"And Mirko, you are not to go to the Zwinger, please remember." On the balls of his feet, Mirko hopped millimeters and hoped for release. His coat, a hand-down from his older brother and too big for him, had to be tamed with a belt fastened on the outside by Adette. It ballooned on either side of the belt's constraint, and Gregor stared down at Mirko with chagrin affixed loosely to his face. Gregor knew Mirko had heard him, but wondered if his warnings held purchase in the boy's mind. "Mirko?"

"Yes?"

"Do you understand?"

"Yes," Mirko said, turning, and making for the door. He had the speed of tiny things, mouse speed, but Gregor caught him just as Mirko's hand reached the knob.

"I mean it, Mirko. The Zwinger is dangerous." Mirko looked playfully into Gregor's eyes and nodded disingenuously. Gregor sighed, "Now go quickly, and be back before dark." The last sentence caught the tail end of Mirko's progress down the stairs, his coat flapping wildly everywhere but the center, where it was tight around the small boy's frame.

The air remained still but it became wind in the face of Mirko's momentum. He dodged people crowding the streets and hopped over people lying down; the city of Dresden was one secret passageway and Mirko was the sole possessor of its blueprints: a knowledge of its trickiest corners, its covert above-ground routes. Mirko took a corner at a sharp angle, narrowly missing a man leaving the post office who meant to look angry but had to focus too much on the balancing act that was his charge of parcels to snarl his face.

Mirko was quick and sprite, able to negotiate avenues that would cause boys twice his size to volley off the walls and boys half his size to lose themselves in the tangle of the busy city center. Across the cobblestones he sped, a hand always outstretched, like a rudder, held against the brick of whatever wall he passed, so he could feel the friction. That one hand, gliding endlessly against the aged stone of ancient buildings, was calloused at the fingertips, but acted to guide Mirko through the city, to steer him in his otherwise seemingly chaotic velocity. In his other hand was always a piece of paper bunched at the center where he held it in a fist, the ends frayed and coming out of his clenched fingers like a bow-tie or a double-sided bouquet of white fanned flowers.

About late-afternoon, Mirko rested his legs by sitting on the steps of the Frauenkirche. He looked up at the building but could not see the cupola.

To Mirko, the people who lived outdoors, as he often wished to do himself, should have been happy. His youthful mind dreamed romantically of sleeping amidst the buildings of Dresden; unlike his actual living situation, sleeping inside of the small cramped apartment with his family, where he felt so outside of the city, Mirko wanted to sleep amidst it. He longed for the freeing life of the men who slept on the stone that most people figured was meant for walking, and who lay in the parks while the buildings made dark shadows of the sky.

Gregor was more practical and somewhat hurt that the hard hours he worked to keep that small apartment were not just unappreciated, but that his little, precocious brother would rather live with the filth of homeless people littering the streets.

"And what of the cold?" Gregor once asked.

"Cold?"

"Winter."

"But there are men out there then, too."

"I know." And for Gregor, the conversation was over.

Mirko, with his final message of the day, his legs now rested, had his senses affixed to the dusk sky of the city, a still-life painting that he did not think of as many miles above Dresden, but part of it. Somehow, it was the city that was making those unnatural beauties of color above him, dyeing the clouds a pink cotton. He approached the steps of a contemporary building with carved vivisecting lines on the stones around the door. He ascended each step with a lunge and knocked on the wooden door set back beyond a stone archway that connected at its apex with a keystone. Behind him, at this hour, there was no movement. The people who had homes were in them, and Mirko knew, was warned by Gregor, that when it became dark, there were many things to be vigilant about. Mirko was nine years old, a short rise from the ground, a child with a pocket full of rattling change while a large population of people hadn't eaten for lack of what rattled in Mirko's pocket. Men laughed at the sound of flapping paper money, used it as wallpaper. As for the coins, there seemed to still be worth in their weight. So he was more careful to look around, to watch. The door opened.

"Mirko Mirko, the Miracle. Hello! And for me, a new message."

Mirko smiled the smile for which he was known and handed Mr. Engel the message wrinkled in his hand.

"Mirko, if you're ever to become a professional in this business, you'll have to learn to keep your documents crisp." Mr. Engel bent down to a knee to deliver his latest lecture. Mirko stood now eye to eye with him and listened intently, though he took no heed to what was being said. He simply smiled and waited for his pay.

"Listen, Mirko, will you come in?"

Mirko looked behind Mr. Engel into his home, and though it wasn't uncommon that he would enter houses or businesses during his day, he knew that time would escape him, as it always had, and he would find himself in the darkest part of night, on his way home quickly, where Adette would be crying endlessly for fear while Gregor sat red-faced and exhausted waiting for his return. Mr. Engel's house seemed welcoming, especially considering that there weren't many houses that still had that sort of prestigious allure in Dresden. From the doorway, receding into a back room, was a red carpet that looked like velvet with small green squares making invisible images in the negative space. Someone, a female, whistled from another room and the smells of roasting and baking that rolled on the back of that whistle summoned him inside. But he knew he had to resist.

"I cannot," Mirko said, without losing his smile, "dark soon."

And as if this was a revelation in its own right, Mr. Engel looked beyond Mirko into the street, then up at the sky, and agreed, "So it is. I am sorry. I suppose I have been so busy that I had not noticed the end of the day. Okay, Mirko, I will not slow you down." He handed Mirko a coin. "Now be on your way before your brother has a belt for you, and mind who you talk to on the way home now. Please, remember Mirko. When you have, and people want, they no longer see *you*. They see what you have."

Gregor had never taken a belt to Mirko. He'd never struck him at all, but Mirko did not want to tarry on the subject; he had delivered his message and had received the final coin of the day, and was eager for his last quick run through the city before he got home.

He nodded as his way of thanks to Mr. Engel and left the building. Watching him go, Mr. Engel shook his head and smiled an unnatural smile. The whistling behind him went on and the smells of the kitchen tickled his stomach. Within seconds, Mirko was tilted at an angle, fighting centrifugal force while rounding a corner, and was gone. Mr.

Engel wished that Mirko was simply running because precocious boys had to run with all of the energy pent up in
their legs, but he heard the necessary coins ringing from
Mirko's pocket for a few blocks more and frowned.

Gregor had had to adopt cautiousness as he'd adopted
his siblings. Bridget had lost consciousness a second time
while Mirko was coming to be born, and the midwife, looking over at the two elder children embracing each other,
swallowed a dry conciliatory gulp in the recess of her
throat. She breathed out forcibly, bowed her head, then
returned to her charge, helping Mirko into the world by
pushing him out, from up to down on Bridget's womb, massaging him into life.

The midwife presented the baby to its mother, but the
mother made no motion. Her face was in the placid ease of
rest, so much so that she could have been presumed to be
sleeping, had not her eyes been open. Mirko was thus devoid of the first intimacy.

Without Bridget to tend to her children, it was up to
Gregor to take on the responsibilities of the home. He was
occasionally assisted by his father's family from Kassel,
who would stay with the children for incalculable amounts
of time—an aunt, then a cousin, then another aunt, be-
grudgingly providing the three children with finances for
food. Though their presence was always felt, in their undulating cycles as caretakers for the small family, they provided no warmth. In their estimation, and in their constant suggestion, they were there out of honor for the
memory of their late relative, Gregor's father, who did not
perish in the war to have his family starve because of a
dead wife and stupid children. It fell then on Gregor to
provide his sister and brother with the comfort of family
that he had learned those early years in their small apartment when their mother would point to the oldest buildings
of the city and tell him they were his.

It was Gregor who would provide them with warmth.

But of course, Gregor was still a boy, and boys show most of their affection by being as mean as they can.

Girls get pinched.

Puppies get punched.

Windows get broken.

It is all done out of a strange love and respect for the world that boys, in their ignorance, hope to control. Like God, with the ambivalent, omnipotent power to create and destroy, boys, having not the function of the former, feel God in their veins by being agents of the latter. And if meanness is the measure by which affection is bestowed, than it is between brothers that the most violent infamy is doled.

"Your name is not even German," Gregor would tease his brother.

"It is."

"No."

"Gregor, it is. Say it is."

"I cannot. Mirko. Mirko. It doesn't even sound German. It sounds silly. Like the English word *miracle*. A little Miracle Mirko."

Mirko would pout his bottom lip, pointing it at his older brother as Gregor continued, "Like *Gregor*. Do you feel the way your tongue moves in your mouth when you say my name? Gre-gor. The hollow sounds your throat makes. This is a German name. Gregor. Try it Mirko."

"No."

"So you agree."

"No."

"Mirko the Miracle."

"Stop it, Gregor. I am German. I know it."

"Of course you are German, Miracle, but your name,
I'm so sorry, is Polish or Irish or British or bloody American. Soot for you."

With Adette, Gregor was much more careful. She represented his mother as she looked just like her, a toy doll replica of the woman whose voice he so longed to hear but never again would. Adette was sensitive, lonely, and introverted. Once, an aunt from Kassel suggested that if it wasn't for the whiteness of her eyes in the darkness of the room, no one would ever know that she was there. Her eyes had the magnificent whiteness of unblemished snow, a child's teeth white, clear and untouched orbs obstructed only at the blue curvature of her frost-bespeckled irises. When Gregor teased her, saying "I'm worried about your eyes, I am afraid they are not getting enough blood," she cried for three hours, which made Gregor very upset. Despite her crying, however, her eyes never bloodshot. They were still just as white as they always were, the only bright beacon that suggested she was there.

Mirko's lively pursuit through the streets of Altstadt was not tempered by the people he nudged or hopped. People shouted at him as he spun them or caused them to jolt to a stop, but their voices could not carry fast enough to his retreating ear, and he never felt punished. What he felt was urgency. His work was to deliver the message bundled in his free-swinging hand from one side of town to the other, then from that side of town back, and so forth. The urgency he felt was not because he took a particular pride in the thriftiness of his work, nor did he realize any importance in the messages he delivered; rather, his urgency came from a license to move quickly, to sprint through the streets and challenge each passing corner. It was adrenaline; the city, his playground.

Mirko spent most of his time outdoors. Not the outdoors of the natural wilderness, but the great outdoors of a wild city, where he would examine and discover what streets went where and how.

He was intrigued and enamored by all that was Dresden from the first time his feet found the ground that supported it; Dresden took off, up like a bird and out like an ocean. A stone ocean of buildings and people and, if he closed his eyes tightly enough, of smells that would waft from here and float by from there. Its streets were crooked as a labyrinth, a dry Venice, filled with mysterious corners and narrow alleys that opened into wide expanses of squares where suddenly a spring of life emerged with moving people. Buildings abutted one another, blossoms of an abbreviated bouquet, to form endless strange edges that ushered pedestrians where the city wanted them to go. Bright green parks quilted elegantly with grey stone, forming a field of seamless color transitions that was the bedrock of Dresden. Architects seemed to wed sculptors in concepts of design, turning simple stone gazebos at the center of roundabouts into Greek temples and common fountains into Holy Grails. Stones, varied in color—from yellow sandstone to deep-streaked marble—found purchase as bricks in the exterior of walls, and altered shades with the day's changing light. And the Elbe, the baptizing blood of the city, moved wisely beneath the bridges that held the city together. And Mirko *was* happy, a boy, running through the streets that quickly became his. It was his, old Dresden. And in a sincere way, he belonged to it, too.

Him it.

It him.

Old Dresden.

Gregor had shared the secret of the Frauenkirche with Mirko, that it was his to run around and around. And while Gregor kept that concept as a memorial to his lost mother, Mirko took the charge seriously, and found himself often rounding the giant ornate church over and over, each revolution like arms around a clock, telling no time. Growing up, he circumnavigated the Frauenkirche hundreds of times but never entered. After Bridget failed to wake, the family never again stepped foot in the building. The secret was outside, around it.

And once, when Mirko was eight, rounding and rounding the church at high speed, a man stopped him, slipped him a note and a coin and said, "You are a fast boy, bring this to Friedrichstadt at the address written. Do you know it?" Without answer, Mirko took what was given him and negotiated his way to his instructed destination with comical speed. With the note delivered, the recipient called after Mirko as he made his way perilously back into the stone wild, telling Mirko to return with a note back to the sender.

This exchange went on for the better part of the afternoon, and when it was over, the two men volleying the boy were on the verge of a highly publicized financial dispute and Mirko was the owner of quite a stack of coins.

Gregor immediately disapproved. "You cannot Mirko. You are too young."

"But it is only running."

"You are too young." Gregor did not want Mirko wrapped up in the world of business. His own work granted him a scorn for money and the intolerable way it was obtained. He wished to be the only provider for the family, a vain pride born from responsibility and an unconscious desire to have Mirko simply be a boy.

But Gregor was no parent. There was little he could do to settle his younger brother, who was infused with a spirit that reminded Gregor of fire. His little body was a wick; his purpose was to burn. Gregor protested Mirko's rattling pockets nightly, despite the benefit they brought to the household, but he eventually conceded. Gregor was adept at recognizing futility, and Mirko was a messenger boy, on fire and burning gladly.

They could no longer rely on the strength of their prayers. The Frauenkirche was beloved to them only for its exterior.

The interior grounds of the Zwinger were the quietest place in Dresden at dusk. That is not to say there wasn't noise or talking. A lonely violin could be heard from the square just outside, moaning in vain for the attention of patrons who might spare something for the player's filling the night with sound. It wasn't a mute quiet, but it was a soundful silence, a reverent communal inhale at the stone walls surrounding the interior garden with darkening clouds above. Those walking the grounds during the day could have felt themselves lovely, perhaps part of a painting, stuck in one pose for eternity on a museum's wall, and content to stand posing for that eternity for onlookers enraptured by the beauty of a place that paint couldn't begin to describe. In the evening, there was sound, but the effect of the atmosphere seemed like silence.

The Zwinger's palatial structure took on the form of an arena, with its bronze-greened roofs atop aging stone; the building was a sort of square, hollowed in the middle to allow the interior grounds to be witness to the open sky. While standing in the middle of the square, framed by the walls of the Zwinger buildings themselves, someone new to Dresden would feel captured there, a random and seemingly secret garden of grass and fountains just beyond the exterior structure where, in the summer, there used to be singers and small orchestras serenading the square with music. Small walkways led to grassy areas, and without any sort of cover, the Zwinger's interior grounds felt like a natural wilderness, a public park, where one could lie on their back and watch the day push the clouds by as the shadows danced from west to east. If it rained, people allowed it to fall. This is the sort of serenity people knew of the Zwinger grounds.

Mirko looked upon the interior grounds from the rim of a fountain. He wasn't resting; he was enraptured. Mirko had never seen the singers and orchestras of the summer. What he saw was what he had always seen: people making the interior grounds their home, people huddled together in clumps on the grass around the fountains, people standing against the stone buildings to block the wind, and people covered with whatever scraps of paper they could find to arm themselves against cold. They were dirty, and their eyes looked sunk and shallow. They never smiled, but looked with remorse at one another and themselves. Mirko did not feel afraid of them, though he was told to beware. He went there almost every evening, after his last message was delivered, and sat on a fountain's rim to watch people prepare for sleep in this portrait bedroom. And of course, this bedroom, wide and green with the falling sound of water and the open sky, surrounded by old brick and bronze-green roofs, seemed much more comfortable a place to sleep than his small apartment.

Perspective tends to rule opinion; the same object viewed from different eyes takes on a different shape, a different color. Mirko looked upon the homeless people lying on the Zwinger grounds as a community of people at one with the city. To him, their reclined figures on the soft grass were comfortable, at ease. From their perspective, they were afraid. Always afraid. Without a suggestion of where their next meal would come, or how they would ever house their families again, the only final attitude was helpless fear. They were families, lying huddled together, the father emasculated as his children starved. They were former teachers. Butchers. Locksmiths. They were carpenters, wounded veterans, boot-blacks. Farmers having sacrificed their land, forced to move into the city.

They would have given anything for a small apartment.

The splashing of the fountain behind him muted the approach of a very thin man who sat down next to Mirko, whose legs dangled a half-meter above the ground. Night was full on now; Gregor would be mad. Still, Mirko was captured, arrested by the serenity common to tragedy. A still, lonely peace in the greatest times of terrible affliction. Moments of clarity that, because of their rarity, seem the crystal, clandestine pieces of heaven that fell when God wasn't looking, which, to most without proper homes that evening, He seemed to never be. Mirko only noticed the man's presence when he made a shuffling sound. Quickly, Mirko turned to him and was frightened. He could get away, as fast as he was, but he did not drop to his feet and run. He stayed still, because when he recoiled in fear of the man's proximity, the man recoiled in kind. The thin man's fear negated Mirko's, so they sat there on the rim of the fountain, looking at each other's eyes. The man's gaze was so vacant that it didn't seem he was looking at the boy, but rather just at his eyes, as if he was looking at the orbs themselves.

Mirko made to say something, but didn't.

The man made to keep silent, which he did.

Someone across the grounds coughed so loudly that it drew Mirko away from the thin man's eyes; he thought the words *Spanish Cold* and it suddenly reminded him that he shouldn't be there, that eventually, there would be more to follow the thin man, like buzzards recognizing that a kin found a corpse. He turned back and the thin man had his hand raised, a completely vacant gesture, harmless, just his hand up in the air, level with his head. Mirko watched the hand, boney and translucent even in the evening, as it hung there, half a wave of hello and half a white flag of surrender. The thin man kept his hand elevated for a moment more, then brought it very slowly to his own cheek, rich with tangled hair, and sighed deeply out as if the sudden shock of tactile sense reminded him that he was alive and that it was not a comfortable remembrance. That one absent action of a man's hand and a man's cheek and a man's sigh and a man's life changed something in Mirko. It wasn't so much his perspective; it was the knowledge of perspective, the knowledge that there was something he did not yet know of the world. Prior to this moment, Mirko, like all small children, knew the world in the microcosm that was his sightline, nothing towered over his eye height. The movement of the thin man's hand gave him the terrible epiphany of maturity: that the world was a big place, bigger than Dresden, more complex than he cared to imagine.

It was the first time Mirko remembered being sad.

But he was a practical boy. Being sad wasn't a state of perpetual anguish; Mirko simply felt the need to extinguish the sadness. Logic told him that if he was sad, he would make up for it by making himself happy.

So Mirko pulled the small column of coins from his pocket and placed them on the centimeters of fountain rim between him and the thin man, dropped to his feet, and ran away, hard against the truths that made the sacred world of ignorance vulnerable.

When Gregor was fifteen, the relatives from Kassel ceased to come, as Gregor was then old enough to work and support his family, which he did. At a local cigarette factory, Gregor checked the quality of cigarettes passing to packaging, but unlike the other workers, who would occasionally grab a bundle for themselves, Gregor did not smoke. The work was constant and tedious in its monotony. Gregor found himself at the factory in the early morning, and would not leave until quite late, when the sun had had enough with the day. He claimed to live there, to Adette, who then had the responsibility of the household, told her that the factory was his true home. That she should see it: unlike the ceiling of their small apartment that seemed to shrink as he grew, the factory's ceiling was part of the sky. He spoke about it lovingly, but there was resentment in the deep tones of his voice. Not yet a man, Gregor was working long hours, dodging the warehouse men who coughed with what they called the Spanish Cold and refusing to listen as they talked of how they were starving—not themselves, not their families, but all of Germany. How they were a starving culture without food and without identity. Smoking their clandestine cigarettes, coughing on Cold, the factory men spoke of how Germany was being squeezed by two giant thumbs at either end, all its moisture being released like a sponge. They felt the country was soon to dry up. But Gregor would not listen. He thought of Adette's white eyes, Mirko's mouse-speed, and his mother, and he worked on.

For good measure, Mirko did a lap around the Frauenkirche on the way home.

Gregor was waiting.

A droplet of flame burned low in the cylinder of a white candle, illuminating Gregor's face only on one side, and only dimly, the shadows streaking across it menacing as he sat and watched Mirko enter. Mirko shut the door quietly behind him and bowed his head, refusing to see Gregor that way. Shadowed. Lit from one side as if half his face was gone.

"I'm sorry," Mirko whispered. At least he thought he did, he wasn't entirely sure that any sound left his mouth.

"Where?" was all Gregor said.

Mirko looked over at Adette, who sat against the wall, her hands overlapping and covering her mouth so tightly it looked like she'd smother herself.

Mirko did not lie. "The Zwinger. Gregor, I..." Gregor raised his hand to stop his brother from continuing; the semblance of the gesture echoed the thin man's and had a similar effect on Mirko. Gregor bowed his head and brought the raised hand to his brow. He shook his head silently back and forth. Mirko knew this much about Gregor: he was not violent, nor was he ever really angry. Rather, he displayed a disappointment that affected him worse than if he would have been beaten. Gregor just breathed, every breath noticeable in the still air of the otherwise silent apartment.

He simply said, "Please."

"Ok," Mirko responded.

Mirko went and sat down in a chair by the fireplace, which still had enough embers in it to glow like the center of the Earth.

"How much have you got today?" Gregor asked. Mirko watched the burning coal pulse a glow, like it too was breathing, and did not answer his brother. "Mirko," Gregor said again, attempting to steal his attention. "Mirko. Where are you?"

Mirko looked over, "Here."

"How much have you got?"

"Nothing."

Gregor sat up straight in his chair. The candle had died its natural death and the small room was lit only by the undulating orange of the embers. Gregor's chest rose and sunk with the beating of the orange light. Mirko's heart followed suit. Adette's tears welled at the bottom of her eyelids. There was a metronomic rhythm to the family's pulse, their blood rushed in chorus.

"Nothing?"

"Nothing, Gregor, I'm sorry."

Gregor switched his tone to concern. "Were there no messages?"

"There were."

"Were you robbed, Mirko? Dear God."

"No, Gregor. I was not robbed."

"Mirko, where is your money?"

An elaborate lie began forming in Mirko's head. He would tell Gregor that he had hidden the coins under a cobblestone somewhere safe, that he intended on saving to purchase a house with a red velvet carpet as regal as Mr. Engel's. Mirko's mind returned there now, guided back by the trace of the smell. He had the lie planned, organized, and ready. "I gave it away. To a man. At the Zwinger. He was hungry." The lie failed and fled his head. The sentences were short with distinct stops between each, gazelles galloping.

For a moment, nothing else was said. The echo of *Zwinger*, with its sharp first syllable, lingered in the air. Gregor wrestled himself to his feet, pointed at Adette, and said, very quietly, "You see her? She is hungry. Where are your alms for her?"

Gregor went and dropped onto his cot, organizing his body in a position it would stay in until the morning, when he would again rise and leave before the sun for the cigarette factory.

Chapter 6

One truth I know is that most assume elderly people's minds are as feeble as their bodies. That assumption is wrong. The mind that is me has the same memories of my younger years; it harbors all of the ships of my latent dreams, no matter the stasis of their sails. The shell around the mind slowed, that is all. And that look you see in the eyes of the elderly is not the vacuous loss of mental faculty; it is the calm acceptance of the consolidation of all the things they've witnessed collated into one resource, a mind at the end of a life. And with the body failing so considerably, the mind is forced to oscillate like a ribbon tied to the end of a stick, up and down in the dry waves of forced remembrance.

Today when my alarm clock shouts, I rise from my bed.

I walk slowly into the kitchen and sit down at the small table that lifts on a hinge up from the wall. Beyond my window, it is again a day at which to marvel. South told me to hold tight, that we had a pretty serious storm coming, the residual of some hurricane that hit the Carolinas pretty hard. As predicted, the sky promises a threat, but it is before the storm. A bright sun shines behind a layer of enormous clouds that blanket the city, a wool cap on a bulb. The sky must be so bright beyond because the fringes of the clouds are transparent and I can see the deep dark centers of rainwater waiting malevolently.

South promised to come over this morning early for breakfast, but his early is not as early as mine. He'll be here in an hour or two. I think South is just as lonely as I am; feels just as undeserving of redemption. Who, though, has the power, the purity, to boldly declare where forgiveness is appropriate? In the year that I've known him, he talks as much about his family in Philadelphia as he insinuates wanting to hear my story. It's like a distant Nirvana, Philadelphia, a place I've never been. A place he refers to as a "shithole paradise."

I want to ask him why he left.

I want to ask why he doesn't go back.

But then I think of my own story, the one I don't want to tell, and think that South must have one as well. A story. A hidden story, lost as a tome in the back of a bookshelf, behind the classics and the beach-read throw-aways, invisible to visitors but thumping like the Tell-Tale Heart.

There are times when I want to be honest with South. We live in the same building, so it's as if nothing I say could ever get out; it would travel between our apartments and stall at the front door. I want to let South know the truth about what happened to me back then, because, well, because I've never had anyone to tell, and withholding it has been a lump in my throat, making it difficult to swallow and breathe. As kind as he's been to me, I feel he deserves to know about the day grey numbers were sunk into my arm. Everything that happened before, and everything that happened after. Sometimes I feel that telling my story to South would be like lancing a blister, opening up the pressure of a vacuum, quelling a baby's crying, making me human again by connecting me with another human. Because that's one thing the camp took away from me, my humanity. Not my faith in it, but my humanity itself. South could be that one person to hear my story, and to confirm it by listening.

People with bad memories always have to be honest. Others will remember what they say even when they do not. My memory is too perfect, so I shroud my truth in silence.

I imagine it: him and me, six beers, and a candle because too much light hurts my eyes, and my long, long conversation, his nodding, and it being all over. I am human again and South gets what he wanted, my story. And the

sun sets, and the lights of the city come on, and everything
is possible once again.

But this is something I will never do.

Because I am a coward.

South will petition in not so many words, but like *his*
secrets, mine will be mine. They will be on the verge of
being told on my tongue, but they will remain mine. If you
hold something to yourself long enough, it becomes part of
you. I knew this when, walking from the market one Sunday, I noticed a tree that had a Gothic iron cage placed
around it as a sapling. As it grew into the massive tree it
is today, the trunk exceeded the boundaries of the iron, and
instead of snapping around it, it consumed the cage. I
walked by that one Sunday, stopped to rest, and admired
the thick tree with iron spears protruding out of it from not
a wound, but a communal place of connection. I've likewise
absorbed my cage. It protrudes from me, and though it is
invisible, I am impaled. South called me a survivor, but I
am not. Living is not the same as surviving. And I am
alive, but I do not survive. I escaped, a fortune I pay for.

I do not hear South come in. I continue to stare out the
window and he fingers white chipping paint from my
kitchen's doorjamb; some of it flutters to the floor like ash,
and rests fragmented.

"See like I told you, right? Big ass storm out there,
yeah? We always get bumped to first class on the shortest
flights."

I turn slowly around, and there is my friend.

CHAPTER 7

One by one the people stepped slowly into the large box of the furniture truck. The truck was an old model, not the most recent Volkswagen 1941 with increased cargo space and plush cushioning in the cab, but an old rusting '35 that sagged on one side due to a bent axel weary from use and had a makeshift ventilator shaft carved from the roof. There was no step into the truck, so the people had to climb or jump, help each other up, or hand children from one to another.

It was raining, the ground sodden with dark reddish mud, a viscous clay that claimed many shoes as people sunk half a foot into it and withdrew to find their foot naked. There was the canopy of forest above them, but it did not do much to prevent the raindrops from finding purchase through the foliage to the ground below. When a drop would hit a helmet, it would splatter in all directions after making a violent *pop*; if it hit the hair of a head, it would cause a momentary startle in the owner of the head, who felt like he was being struck by something more solid than water.

The people stood in two very straight lines, shivering, and waiting to board the furniture truck. Their eyes all focused down and most held their arms crossed in feeble protection from the precipitation. A dog barked angrily, his body looking thinner than it did before the rain with the wet mopped hair pasted to his body. Though the darkness, the interior of the truck seemed oppressive and final, and though it was becoming packed to capacity, the people waiting in line saw it as a refuge from the striking rain that was almost painful.

If any of them noticed that two of the four tires of their transport were flat, they made no mention of it.

Goaded by the insistence of the men in charge, the truck's open mouth pulled with the magnetism of a black hole, each person in his turn, climbing in to appease event horizon. A father climbed into the truck ahead of his small son and bent low to lift him in, but the boy slipped on the watery mud and fell face first to the ground. The line of people stopped behind him but did not bend down to help. Rather, they looked around sheepishly at one another. The boy stayed still for a moment, as if he was there permanently, to become a fossil, then pulled his little blond head from the ground and tried to wipe the mud from his eyes but his hands were likewise covered, and what he wiped, he replaced.

The boy's father made to jump down from the truck and help his son, but before he could, he looked over at the soldiers, who had taken notice of the fallen boy and who very slightly moved their fingers up and down the length of the triggers on their rifles. It was a subtle movement, the flat fingerprint pad of the finger, gloved in leather, traveling almost imperceptibly along the length of the lever. But the father noticed it. He hesitated.

"For shame," cried an officer, who walked quickly to the back of the furniture truck, his knee-high boots polished mirror-like and making sucking sounds as they entered and withdrew from the mud. "For shame you do not help this boy!"

It was evident in the way that the other soldiers looked at their toes on the heels of this admonition that the officer was the Commander of the regiment. He made his way quickly over to the boy, glancing back and forth at his soldiers with disapproval. When he got to the boy, he went to a knee there in the mud, spoiling his wet but otherwise unblemished pants, and lifted the boy from his position on the ground to his feet. The boy's lifted body made the same sucking sound as the Commander's boots. From the back of the truck, the boy's father reached in a fast jerky movement toward the ground at the moment the Commander touched his son, but quickly retarded his progress, wise to know that if he came between the Commander and his intent, the fingers of the surrounding soldiers, dancing on the triggers, would rest with pressure.

The Commander used a handkerchief to wipe the mud from the boy's face. The boy stood there staring at the Commander, who smoothed back his blond hair, leaned in, and whispered something into his ear. The boy smiled and the Commander responded with a genuine charming smile of his own that looked the exact reflection, from one set of blue eyes to another. In another situation, it might have been surmised that the Commander and the boy were father and son, but it was not another situation. It was that situation. He lifted the boy into his arms and stood up in the same fluid motion, and, holding the boy close to his breast, with the same charming smile, addressed the soldiers in attendance. "A boy fell in the mud," he said, looking back and forth, above the heads of his receptive audience. Even the dog became quiet. The boy's smile had gone. "If ever again I see a boy fall in the mud and he is not retrieved and cleaned by the nearest soldier, that soldier will be shot. In succession, each soldier nearest the boy will be shot until the boy is righted and cleaned. Please let me make this clear," he said, the charming smile beaming more brightly against the huge drops of falling rain in painful juxtaposition, "no boy shall ever stay stuck in the mud."

The patter of rain sounded like footsteps in the forest, making the people in line feel always surrounded by shifting running things, animals circling, buzzards waiting. Still skin, appetizing.

The Commander lifted the boy into his father's waiting arms and said to the man, "I am sorry for the barbarism of my men." The boy's father nodded, shocked at the display of civility by his captor. There was a moment of tense silence as the muddy boy settled into his father's arms and the Commander looked around to the rest of the congregation. He stood almost as a priest, as reverent as he was revered, at the pulpit of an evangelical summit, pondering the best rhetorical method to inflate the price of Holy Water.

The Commander climbed up into the furniture truck and faced his soldiers and the rest of the twitching people waiting to board. "These are our prisoners," he said, "but we are not monsters. Know that we will be judged not by how we handle our friends, but by how we treat our enemies. With respect, we've temporarily taken their freedom, but we shall never take from them their dignity." The soldiers made no reaction but stood still, listening. The Commander looked back and forth from each of his men, then looked up at the canopy of leaves. His one knee was muddy and the handkerchief he used to clean the boy's face was still in his hand. He then turned sideways to speak to the prisoners both in the truck and waiting to enter. "I am ordered to maintain you. If I do not, I, myself, will be shot. I do not know you, but I do not see you as my enemy. I see you as my charge, given to me by those commanding me. I know there is nothing I can say to comfort you, as upturned as your lives are, but be content to know no harm will come to you so long as you follow the instructions of me and my men."

He gestured to the inside of the truck, "Though this truck has no windows or seemingly appropriate ventilation, our options for transport are few, and the time of transport is short; you will arrive at your final destination safely and soon. I apologize for any inconvenience."

He turned once again to his men and said, "To understand one's enemy, one must first recognize his humanity." With that, the Commander dropped from the furniture truck and walked quickly back into the crowd.

The rest of the people made their way into the furniture truck, comforted a little by the Commander's speech. When the last person had entered, a young soldier grabbed a rope that hung from the truck's back door and pulled it down, leaving them in total darkness. The rain hit the top of the furniture truck's box and sounded like hammering. The young soldier locked the back door shut and returned to the Commander, where he was beckoned.

A large hose was then attached from the exhaust pipe of the cab to the makeshift ventilation shaft in the top of the truck's box, where it was sealed airtight. The engine was turned on.

The Commander had lost the charming smile as the young soldier approached.

"What is your name soldier?"

"Mirko Erinnerung, Sir," he said, standing straight with his heels together and his arms flat at his sides. The Commander nodded, as if they knew each other. They did not. But the Commander made it a point to know the names of his men; naming was a form of control, and calling a person by his name provided an intimacy that in times of conflict, would translate to loyalty. The Commander took an inventory of the soldier's face and connected it with its name.

"Yes," replied the Commander, "Mirko Erinnerung. Put your ear to the truck. When you hear nothing, you may open it again."

Barely Plenty

Chapter 8

There were two types of prisoners who entered the camp: the doomed and the permanent. What always struck me was the way the tracks entered the gates from the outside and ran the length of the camp until the entire train fit just perfectly, and the tracks just stopped. It was engineered that way, perfectly. The end of the line. No switch, no detour. Trains go as far as their tracks, and when the tracks end, so too does the journey.

Departing the train, two distinct lines formed as passengers were sifted and sorted by ranking officers and doctors who would briefly examine each person and point either left or right. Little was ever said; most often, it was a minute gesture of the head, this way or that way, and the new arrivals would corral into their respective lines, stealing glances at the other line and wondering which was lucky, theirs or ours. Both lines went to the showers. If you were of the line that went to a shower on the left, your last glimpse of daylight would be the moment before you entered, an almost always very bright sun that caught your eye just before the door jamb shaded it forever. If you were sent to the shower on the right, you were *permanent*. I still remember how the prisoners were called *permanent*. As if they would always be there, as if they were fixtures, statues of stone, four hundred men to a bunker, completely and totally and always there. I suppose I am permanently there, too. For now, at least.

Maybe it was a way of keeping them hopeful. If they felt permanent, perhaps they would resist nothing, in the hope that their docility would reap survival.

Maybe it was a sick twist of language, to call something with a truncated timeline static.

Maybe it was for contradiction's sake, for nothing (no one) is truly ever permanent.

Maybe it was literal, they might have been expected to stay and work for the rest of their lives.

Or maybe, it was simply true, in the ashes fertilizing the ground.

Permanently there. I am here, but I am also there. Lombard South wouldn't understand this, so I don't even mention it to him. He is a practical man, incapable of reconciling how a man can be in more than one place at the same time. But a man can be. It's as if I walked out of a sculpture of myself, lifelike and limestone, standing in stride, and kept on; that copy of me, forever and always there.

Permanently.

And every once in a while, I'll feel a breeze that no one else does, and it'll shiver me in a place that's not my body; it'll take my breath when it leaves. It'll carry on its back a smoky smell, similar to the kind coming from bar-b-que restaurants that pump their aromas temptingly onto the sidewalk, but this smoky scent does not cause salivation. It will reek of false salvation. Of people dissipated into the air. The breeze will swirl around me, through me, and for a second, I'll stop dead in my tracks, and breathe in deep through my nose, to smell the smoke that becomes a film on the back of my tongue, where the buds are the most bitter. And I'll know that the breeze is blowing where I am, other than here.

CHAPTER 9

Gregor awoke but was barely awake. He coughed a little into his balled fist and followed it with a deep echoing bellow from the bottom of his chest. The cough convulsed his entire body so that he flopped up with each heave and fell back down on the cot, like a fish fighting for air.

The noise woke Mirko. Adette had been awake, watching Gregor from the side of the cot; when Mirko looked at her, she shook her head. Her white eyes stuck on Mirko while her head shifted back and forth in the dawn light, causing her eyes to volley from each side of her sockets in a way that unsettled Mirko. She smoothed back Gregor's hair, though he absently flung his hand to prevent her from doing so. He was awake but it was difficult to consider him conscious and Adette kept close to him, unafraid of illness. Outside, a cock announced the day and the slow parade of people made their way where they were going—all components of the world en-route to their functions in the world; their steps spinning the planet.

Gregor had woken up this way for the better part of two weeks, in cacophonous convulsions that shook the entire apartment and woke his young siblings. Despite this, Gregor would still eventually rise and lethargically gather himself. Closing the door behind him, a cough would replace his normal goodbye.

On the stove, the tea kettle shouted its internal struggle and Mirko went over to it. He poured three cups of tea for Gregor, Adette, and himself. Into Gregor's mug, he dripped the last of their honey. Mirko brought the mugs for Gregor and Adette over to Gregor's cot and placed them on the wooden stand by his head. They sat there and steamed. He was afraid of getting any closer to Gregor; he had heard of the Spanish Cold from Gregor himself, about how men at the cigarette factory would start to cough, and that people thought it was just because they were stealing too many cigarettes; but that cough would turn into a thick mucus the men would spit to the factory floor. Then, a few weeks later, they simply didn't come to work, and people stopped talking about them.

When Mirko was told these stories, he imagined the men at home, coughing thick cigarette smoke, shivering and their eyes bloodshot. He knew nothing of Spain, but by the descriptions of its Cold, he thought it must be an ugly place. Gregor's playfully horrible depictions of the symptoms were to tease his most impressionable little brother, though Gregor did all he could to avoid the mucus spittle in dark piles all over the floor of the factory that lived with disease. Still, there was always the chance that eventually, he would mirror the missing men. So he told Mirko the stories of disappearing coughing people, hoping to abate his own fear with the fascination of his brother.

Mirko leaned down and shook Gregor by the shoulder, "Gregor. Brother. It is dawn. Will you get up?" Gregor did not open his eyes. His breath sounded wet. He switched from his left side to his right, trying to find a cool place on the cot. He was at the same time unforgivingly hot and shivering the small twitches of little, wet dogs.

Honey was a rarity. Mirko had gotten a small portion of it as a gift from one of his wealthier customers, one that had big cigars and a big belly and no hair save for a bit in a horseshoe that curved around his temples and met in the back of his head, where it sat plastered with grease that made it always look as if the man had been rained upon. This wasn't a reward for Mirko, but a show of power. In the way that the rich dole out alms to seem the saints of the sufferers, the wealthy man wished to show the people who watched the crass display of bestowing the well-loved messenger boy with a gift of honey.

It was a business expense, as are all appearances.

It was done in broad daylight, in public. Like an execution.

Mirko placed a little in Gregor's tea every morning, as if sweetness could defeat sickness.

"Gregor," Mirko said again, a little more urgently. He was worried about Gregor's job, but he was more worried for Gregor. In some sense, if Gregor was able to carry on as usual, then naturally, he would be okay. For Gregor not to rise and begin his journey to the factory was proof that something was truly wrong. This prospect was enough to haunt Mirko into his day. Gregor was a symbol of stability, of rational constancy. He was a fixed structure, like an old church, strong in the same spot, certain for centuries. His sickness was a startling nuance for Mirko, who cocked his head at it like a confused dog, unaware of how to react when the commonplace was replaced with the out-of-place. Gregor was in the foreground of the still life, Mirko's keystone cornerstone grenade pin. A brother, but also, by virtue of absence, a father.

Apparently, Gregor's illness haunted Adette as well, who motioned Mirko away from the bed. The two younger siblings walked to the other side of the apartment near the fireplace.

"Mirko, he cannot go to work," Adette said, biting her lip and kneading her hands into each other.

"No."

"Do you see it is getting worse?"

"Worse?"

"The way he is. Mirko, Gregor has the Cold." The sudden realization that Adette's assumptions mirrored his own made them completely true. Gregor had the Spanish Cold; he hadn't been able to dodge the dark piles of factory spit. But he was sure Gregor would be okay. They had honey.

"What do I do?" he asked Adette, who, now the eldest sensible sibling, was in command.

"You must go to the factory, Mirko. You must go there and tell them that Gregor will not be able to work today. Tell them he is sick."

She looked out of the apartment's small window and touched her hair. Her fingertips loosened a renegade lock from a tie, and it sickled in a curl on her cheek.

"And what if they do not care he is sick?"

Adette's face forged into an expression to that point underrepresented in her lifetime, that of anger. "Then tell them it is their factory that made him this way."

The Yenidze Cigarette factory was massive and peculiar. Its clean stone walls piled up and back as far as Mirko could look, which made the building seem eternal in a dreadful way. From enormous thin towers stretching to point at the clouds came their own clouds, black and organic, twisting into themselves with vulgar contortions. But what prevented Mirko from distracting his gaze enough to enter and find the foreman was the enormous multi-colored glass dome that caught sun and sprinkled bits of painted light in elegance at his feet. It was not how he had thought of a factory. The dome was built similarly to that of the Frauenkirche; but unlike Altstadt's sandstone cupola, the Yenidze factory's pummeling smoke struck at the sky and nearly hid the true magnitude of what its translucent colored vault hoped to conceal. In all of Dresden, it was the one place that seemed to not be born of Dresden.

Mirko did not say this to the foreman of the cigarette factory when he told the man of Gregor's illness. The foreman knew of the Spanish Cold, he had lost a great deal of men to it, but because of that, he could not quarantine anyone or allow them to be absent because of the illness. The rapid loss of men doomed the factory's production and if the factory did not meet demands, the demands would be given to another factory and he, along with the other men, sick or not, would be out of a job. It was his intention to not walk through the parks or the Zwinger grounds with a shamed countenance. He did not want to be reminded of where he might end up by a simple distant twist of fate, represented by a deep bellowing cough and dark piles of spit.

He told Mirko that Gregor comes to work, or has no work.

The place smelled like smoke—not cigarette smoke, but locomotive smoke; a thick pungent penetrating odor that Mirko recognized from Gregor's coat. He smacked his lips together and could taste the smell, his senses confused. The foreman left Mirko alone after his last word and lumbered off into the heat of the machines, limping a little, and scratching at his forearm. The foreman's forearms were red with raised bumps. Mirko watched him go for a moment, then considered the building. What occurred to him was that here was where his brother Gregor had spent the days of his life since Mirko was old enough to know he went anywhere at all. This building with the steel girders crossing the ceiling like the heavy contrails of airplanes crisscrossing the sky, its loud machines moving along, its human counterparts sweating a constant perspiration, its dome, from the inside, constricting at its highest point in what seemed suffocation; it was Gregor's place of business, his second home, and what made him lie on a cot coughing. Full of component parts, it was one heavy organism, all at once all at work, producing small sticks for which Mirko could not comprehend the fascination. He'd seen cigarettes, but now, comprehending what it took to produce them, it seemed an awful ugly waste and a lot of senselessness only for men who wanted to breathe fire.

Mirko knew he should sprint home, tell Gregor what the foreman had said, then return to Altmarkt for whatever messages that needed to go wherever. Instead, Mirko walked slowly into the depths of the factory, in reverence of the moving parts and frightened in the way that big things frighten. Some men had faces almost as young as his, and they watched him longingly as he walked by. Something would screech. Something would grind. The sounds were unnatural to Mirko, fabricated. They sounded like the roaring of an animal whose bones were steel and whose voice was agitated, hoarse, and menacing. Dim lights, soot-covered, flashed distant colors in coordination with a whistle or the movement of an erratic metal arm. It was engineered perfectly, each part in its place, designed to operate as it was programmed. A vast factory that did what it was told, and had men moving the parts, though they knew not what those parts did. It made him think of a line in the Bible, taught to him by Adette, who would give brief halfhearted lessons of scripture in the evenings. *They know not what they do.*

He approached a machine that had a heavy press, which came down hard upon white paper, emitting a plume of steam. Each time it descended, a loud *clunk* would indicate it was locked tight and the steam would billow out and upon itself. A heavyset man repeatedly pulled a lever to activate the mechanism, time and time again. Once for each of his breaths. Mirko went right up to him just as the heavy press came down and tugged on his coat, smiling up at him as the man turned and looked down. Mirko felt a jurisdiction with the man. He was the beloved messenger boy, Mirko the Miracle, and all were generally content to see him.

"What? Boy. Who are you?" The man turned to face Mirko head on. "What is this? You boy, you can't be here. What—"

"Honey."

"What?"

Mirko started away.

"Wait. What? Honey?" the man said. "What, boy? Honey?" But Mirko was at a full sprint, heading the way he had come, out of the factory and out where the air was cleaner than it had ever smelled. He had mistaken the worker for the rich man; the two looked impossibly similar. Mirko felt the smoke smell grasping to his jacket, so he ran faster to shake it. Behind him, the organism lived on.

Mirko could think of no reason to deliver the foreman's message to Gregor. He did not want Gregor to ever return to the factory. Gregor was ill at home, wrestling with a restless sleep that was constantly interrupted by coughs. Money was important, in some esoteric way that older men knew, but in what way exactly, Mirko was inept to know. What he did know, was that he didn't want Gregor to go back to the factory, so he did not return home with the warning. He went instead to Augustusbrüke, to watch the Elbe.

Its current awoke in him a hunger. It was blue flowing, on its way to somewhere, perhaps everywhere. In no other symbol than flowing water can a child's conception of the world be recognized. It moves; it is permanent, infinite, omnipresent and potent, a baptismal rite of passage that carries imagination through the cities and to the oceans. The river had no beginning and no end, a liquid Ouroboros. And though Mirko did not feel these things specifically, being too young to recognize those sorts of concepts, he nevertheless took a special consideration of the river. The Elbe slithered through his city, winding a divide between the old of Altstadt and the new of Neustadt, and was straddled by the ornate sutures of bridges that seemed to hold Dresden together.

He stood in the middle of such a bridge. The beautiful Augustusbrüke. From there his vantage included the old enduring durable skyline, the Elbe and its freedom, and the modernity of the north bank. People crossed the cobbled street, almost unconcerned with the passing vehicles. Mirko heard their chatter, their redundant commentary. People were aggravated on the surface, but that aggravation was a reaction to a fear below. Soon, something would have to budge. This frightened the people of Dresden even more than embargo, than French occupation to the north, than military emasculation. The image in every man and woman's mind in the city was of an eminent budge. Germany was backed into a corner, castrated, and was forced to wear the dunce cap of Europe; it would only be a matter of time before the dog bit back. They knew it, the people of Dresden, and as much as they wanted to regain their national pride, the wounds of the war were still stretched and open, available for infection. Dresden was in trepidation with the thought of a budge, a change that would widen the wound and perhaps drag a blade once again over the world.

All Mirko could think about was Gregor's cough and that awful factory. He was too short to see over the bridge's stone railing, the top of which looked like a castle's embattlement wall crossing the river, so he stood on the tops of his toes gracefully and pulled himself up onto the ledge with the impossible strength only children seem to possess, and sat. Mirko dangled his legs over the ledge above the water, while people went where they were going, while messages were left undelivered, and while his older brother's lungs filled.

He rubbed his flat palm against the smooth stone of the railing. His mind brought him the fearful reality of Gregor's illness. Despite his thoughts, his field of vision provided him with views of beauty that contradicted the image of Gregor lying prostrate and supine. The Spanish Cold and the Frauenkirche. These opposing images pitted Mirko against himself, a young boy yet, at the crossroads everyone would walk, the bridge where one first realizes that the world is a beautiful place and that the world is an ugly place. Where people are good and people are bad. Where, as day is distant to night, so too is the divide between what makes the world spin, and what aims to pull it apart. Mirko was on the middle of a bridge, between two entirely different worlds. It was a children's bridge, *the* children's bridge; where, upon the distant bank, he would grow to see above the railing, and everything that showed.

It was a one-way bridge.

It had a river flowing underneath.

Mirko returned home late that afternoon and could not convince Gregor no matter what he tried. Adette had asked Mirko what the foreman said and Mirko, not knowing any other way, was honest. Gregor was not asleep. Upon overhearing, he rose slowly from bed, with his hand still over his face, and proceeded to get ready to leave. Mirko pleaded with his older brother, giving him the terrible descriptions of the factory despite the fact that he knew Gregor had seen it many more times than he had.

Mirko mentioned the press, the men sweating and coughing, and all the machines as loud as any sound he had ever heard. He told Gregor not to return to that place, as if he commanded authority over Gregor's actions; Mirko was surprised with the sternness of his own voice. Gregor never responded. He simply put on his coat and left.

CHAPTER 10

"You know what gets me? What gets me are people who nod their heads at things they already know." South shrugs his shoulders like even *he* doesn't understand what he's carrying on about.

Somehow, we've ended up in Miami.

"People who nod their heads, you know? Old man, you're listening, yeah?"

I'm afraid to nod. So I say, "What?"

South tries to nonchalantly point at one of the other people in the tour group, though his finger couldn't be any more obvious, at the business end of his extended arm. He leans over and whispers, "Like this guy." He's a head taller than me, so his whisper travels over me. An elderly woman in a Hawaiian-print shoulder-to-ankle muumuu on the other side of me looks over and makes a face that suggests she'd like to tell South to *shhh*, but this isn't the time nor the place. She and I catch eyes and it's almost as if she expects me to quiet my friend, because we are both old and in that, have some sort of bond. Wishing South would speak more loudly brings me great joy.

"So watch this guy, he nods every time the tour guide says something, like he already knew it and we're wasting his time."

The guide mentions a large number and points to a bronze-green little girl's statue that lies on the ground in the middle of our tour's circle wailing for help that she can't see, with her carved-out hollow eyes. We stand around her, not helping. It's amazing how we idolize horror. Sure enough, the guy South pointed to nods his head in affirmation.

"There he goes," South says. "Nods his head every fucking time, yeah?"

"Maybe he knows," I say.

"Knows shit," replies South. "If anybody should be nodding because he knows, it's you, yeah? I mean, who's this guy?" He taps me on the left forearm. The grey numbers underneath my shirt sizzle. South's accent isn't as foreign in Miami as it is in D.C. There are a lot of rich New York and Philadelphia transplants, snowbirds, here. Florida is drug rehabs and retired Jews, South said, when he was trying to convince me to go on the road trip with him to see other memorials, as if the fact would make it easier for me to say yes. Egrets play in the expected puddles of the once-a-day rains. They don't look up at us from the memorial's fountain, or the puddles surrounding; they squat in the water, and beat their wings like children in the ocean, making their own little waves.

We take cover in a narrow hallway that leads to the center of the memorial as a rain momentarily becomes more violent. Most of us in the group are elderly, so out of respect, South waits and is the last in the hallway, dripping. The tour guide tells us that it'll most likely stop in about fifteen minutes. He says that in fifteen minutes it'll be as sunny as you could ever imagine it. I imagine South dripping wet but standing in the direct sunshine, as if he'd been playing with the egrets.

The hallway we're standing in is concrete but has slits in the stone that allow sunlight to slash through in crooked angles. From these slits, rain enters, and finds purchase in crooked angles on our shirts as we try to dodge it. I stand perfectly still and a rain line appears across my chest diagonally from my shoulder to my hip. South points his finger, tracing the line and says, "You got wet." And we laugh like madmen while the tour guide makes a sour face at us and, in the apathetic way that tour guides of tragic sites drone on as if exhausted by the repetition of their information, points at the stained-glass yellow star on the ceiling, and translates *Jude* for the group from the original German.

My first concern was sitting in a car for long amounts
of time. I imagined motion sickness, restlessness, the fre-
quent need to urinate. I imagined sitting in the seat next
to South as he played music I couldn't stand and drove too
fast. The prospect of thousands of miles between memorials of something I was trying to forget seemed the least entertaining prospect for me.

My next concern was that I had never left D.C. Doing
so after so many years and now as an elderly man seemed
foolish in the absolute.

And finally, I did not want to break my routine. Ever
since the camp, I have been strict about my routines. Waking up, eating, staring out of the window. I do these things
according to a schedule as if the schedule itself was etched
on my arm and a violation of it would cause infection. This
would throw my order into disarray. It would rearrange
everything I took so long to organize by letting things sit.

But South was persistent.

"You sit around here staring out the window all day
anyway," he said. "Why not stare out the window of my
car?"

"I cannot, Lombard. It is too far."

"It feels like it's too far because you've never been.
Maybe it'll feel like it's close when we get there."

"Lombard—"

"Don't 'Lombard' me, Old Man, yeah?"

"Lombard—"

"Listen. I've got a full pension and a full tank of gas. I
don't teach another class until winter, let's pick up. When's
the last time you ever did anything like, exciting like?"

I checked the clock on the wall.

"I haven't. Oh, I don't know, Lombard."

"I'll do the driving. We'll stay in motels. Separate rooms if you want to mope around, wake up early, and stare out the window."

"I'm tired."

"How much energy does being driven around take?"

I shrugged because I really didn't know.

"You hear about the guy who up and quit his job and left his family and spent the next ten years of his life just driving around?" I shook my head because I really hadn't heard. "He's probably still out there, yeah?"

"Yeah, Lombard."

"Maybe we'll meet him."

I agreed to go after telling myself that I'd do it for him. I told myself that South needed the trip, that getting away was *his* need. He, conversely, probably thought he was doing something sweet for an old man. A survivor. A line on his bucket list to canonization. A step toward his own vain contrition. So with all of our contradictions, we set out on a Sunday morning, on a road trip to see the memorials in cities all over the country. I didn't realize what I had agreed to until we were first in the car, and in the reflection of the windshield, I could see the trees around me, moving by too quickly. South had a pile of maps fastened together with a rubber band, a smile as wide as the impending highway, and a box of cassette tapes, which he thought sounded better than CDs. I had no opinion, though I noted his car only had a cassette tape player.

Maybe I agreed to go because South is a difficult man to say no to. Maybe because if he was going, I wasn't prepared to watch him leave without me.

Just like the flame in Baltimore, in Miami, they used the bodies of people to make up the sculpture. They are green, and tangled together; their faces all in agony. I want to tell the tour guide that this is not how it really was, that there were no such faces there. What is true, is that people had no expressions on their faces, not those of agony or joy. Perhaps fear at first, but eventually, the Permanents had blank faces, drawing thinner and more sunk, but always blank. I want to tell him that when you are tired, exhausted, and hungry, you do not waste energy on facial expressions. But telling him this would do no good; he would just look at me, bored by his job, and say, *What do you want me to do, change the statue?* So I don't say anything.

The bodies tangle together to make a hyperbolically large forearm and wrist; protruding from it is a giant green hand that reaches for salvation while the rest of the body is submerged and sinking. The monument is huge and garish—Floridian—not like the subtlety of Baltimore's flame. From the street, the giant green hand seems to rise from nowhere, connected to a Giant emerging. I am almost embarrassed by it; I look around, sheepishly, hoping no one sees, and wonder what the symbol is supposed to suggest. Reaching perhaps. The Giant emerging. The tangled agony of permanent people.

I don't know. South kicks stones around and is restless. The rain stops and we exit again into the center courtyard. The egrets have new playgrounds, and the tourists' cameras click click click.

My friend is intrigued by what happened but I don't know why. He still doesn't ask to hear my story. On the long drive down, I was sure he would. He said things like, "Fucking traffic, yeah?" and, "Jesus Christ this road is long, pardon the expression. Oh. Wait. Never mind," and, "You hungry again yet?" But never, "So Old Man, what happened to you in the camp, you know, specifically," or "Can you tell me what it was really like now?"

We leave Miami going north because there's really no other choice.

When we stop, he swallows half-masticated bites of hamburgers and cola to "keep myself awake, yeah?" and I pick at a bag of chips. I'm never really very hungry. He doesn't ask but I want to tell him. I want to say, "Lombard, here is my story," because my life is an unread book, and the soiled, creased pages of it reek of a stuck story. I think South is a good enough friend to hear it through, to not judge me. To not shake his head too much at what I tell him. I think it would do me good too, reading myself, at night, South tucked in to the chin at a roadside motel, the grandfather I never was. Him lulling on the edge of sleep and my life erasing backwards from then to now, releasing me. But I do not think I will be able to, honestly. There are simply some sounds my vocal cords cannot make. My job is to sit still and look at the different ways different cities memorialize the same thing, which I do.

Chapter 11

The sky was inconsistent with the temperature. Above was clear-cloudless, a distant but bright sun; but down on Earth, somewhere on its surface, it was very cold. The permanent prisoners huddled in a roll call line, one man's front a meter from the previous man's back. For the purposes of body heat, they wished to be closer to one another, but knew their companions did not generate any readily shareable heat themselves. They were under-dressed, the garments on their shoulders too thin, some of their feet shoeless. Veins were visible through the skin, especially on the feet, where they protruded a rude blue, trapped between the skeletons they all were and the thin skin that cloaked them. Most hung their mouths open, so that when their jaws trembled, their teeth wouldn't chatter and welcome the unwelcomed attention of the guards. The trick was to make themselves as small as possible without seeming small. Truly small people didn't remain perma-nent for long. But to seem small was the daily, silently concurred-upon agreement, to make as little noise as hu-manly possible, for a human.

For people so viscously dulled to numbness, the one sense of the five that didn't seem to recess was hearing. Eventually, nerve endings stopped sending tactile signals to the brain, perhaps to save energy in the synapses; the eyes could not focus, but dilated in and out; the tongue and the nose, intimately linked by the throat, received nothing out of the nothing given. But sound was still perceived, loud sounds most effectively, so orders to march or stand or kneel were interpreted and heeded without so much as the stutter of a small second, missed in a moment.

The men stood erect—their collarbones, hangers on a curved coat rack—for at least an hour every morning while the Commander leisurely arrived and looked through his papers in the front of a truck. If they were to look, the Permanents would see his dark hat unmoving through the windshield. But they never looked. It was his eyes, only, that moved over the words of his documents. In the extreme weather of winter, he'd sit with the heat of the truck off, entertaining the concept of cold, each of his breaths fogging a plate of cloud on the windshield in front of him that would rescind from its edges until he breathed out again, like a pulsing ghost heart. He seemed to be always waiting for something, though he didn't have the nervous mannerisms of an anxious man. His tarry was punctual, however, an hour on the hour, engineered with the same strict brilliance that kept the camp running without so much as a whisper of rebellion or the question of who was in power. The whole game of it.

This was Mirko's first realization when he entered the camp a week before and was assigned guard duty for a section of bunkers: just how well-organized the outfit was. The sheer size of the grounds, the precise execution of layout, the unobstructed views and ominous innuendo of brick buildings just beyond the trees, enough to keep an angry man quiet. The fasting practice, more aimed at breaking spirits than maiming bodies. The life of a place surviving on snuffing life. It was effective. Plain, brilliant, and effective. Mirko was impressed by the organizational engineering of the camp, regardless of its cruelty. To the spoilers go the victories. His responsibility was three bunkers in a row, in the corner of camp, twelve-hundred men, against a right angle of barbed wire hanging from curved stone pylons that looked like frail hunchbacks at night. He couldn't see it, but the knowledge of the wires' voltage almost made them glow. An optical illusion, an innocuous delusion. Simply brushing against them would provoke the final pupil dilation to wide black. His bunkers were in the corner, flanked on two sides by instantaneous death.

The Kapo of his bunkers stood in the front of the line nearest Mirko, waiting as the rest of the men did for the

Commander to leave the cold confines of his truck to initiate the roll call that would precede the day.

It was easy to spot the Kapos; they were always a bit taller than the rest of the Permanents. It wasn't that they were picked for Kapo duty because of their height, but a prisoner working for the guards was awarded a certain measure of benefit, which usually translated in less sores on their feet, a larger portion of food ration, and less physical work; all of which resulted in better posture and ultimately, a taller figure. Mirko's Kapo did not seem tall, however. He was a short man, dressed every day in a dark grey blazer made of rough frieze, which hung far below his waist and had a pocket on the upper left breast. His head was shaved, like the rest, but there was a noticeable cowlick that was a maelstrom in the highest point of his skull. Mirko could see it because the man was so small; the cowlick seemed to spin into the depths of the Kapo's brain. He had the physique and size of a small boy, but it was evident in the Kapo's face that he was a man. Perhaps a young man, but not a child. There were creases on his face where the years had dug furrows. His fingernails were thick and cropped right to the edge of his fingertips; he kept them that way by chewing them off. Mirko assumed the Kapo figured that losing one's grooming was the first step in submitting one's civility, and, of course, the chewing tantalized his salivary glands. He had the inexplicable eyes of a wise man, simply a knowing look, which was intimidating only in the potential depth of storage behind them. If Mirko could guess, he would guess that the Kapo worked the land: his cowlick bucolic. But Mirko couldn't guess.

Mirko was exhausted. His body hung about the bones with an effortless lethargy. He was still young, twenty-two, and full of a reckless potential energy beating at the walls of his body, demanding to be kinetic. But it was as if he could only move his limbs in slow motion, like when being chased by a predator in a dream. He had aged beyond the days he had lived and was prematurely in the subtle slow days of old age, when exhaustion substitutes the audacity of energy.

He had been at the camp for only a week, far less time than any of the Permanents he was tasked to supervise, but it still took the energy from his body, sucked it straight into the ground. Almost as if he was unable to distribute his weight on both feet, Mirko leaned on one foot until fatigue almost crippled it, then he'd switch to the other, and so on. He did not spend a lot of time speaking to the other guards. They all seemed hard and direct, stuck in the mud and happy to be knee-deep in the Earth; there was a gang-like quality to them, fearful and distrusting of new recruits. They watched him and would suddenly become silent when he entered an area where they congregated, as if he were an unwelcomed burden that threatened to tell. Deep down, through all the façades, they were all afraid someone *would* tell. Something about the new young guard told them that he was prone to running. Runners were a liability.

But there, early in the morning, with the distant sun a sky lighthouse and the winter settling in to provoke hung mouths and silent chatter, Mirko had to stand and wait for the Commander to appear, just like the Permanents.

The Kapo leaned in toward Mirko's back, which was just a few feet ahead of him and said, "It's so awfully hot today." It was obvious that Mirko was uncomfortable, the way he switched back and forth on his feet.

Mirko turned his head and pointed his nose to his shoulder. He wondered if he could pretend that he hadn't heard the Kapo speak. It was true that some Kapos were on regular speaking terms with their guards, but Mirko did not intend on carrying on any such tradition, and as far as he was concerned, if this Kapo thought he would, he was wrong. Mirko grunted as an acknowledgment of the man's statement and a warning to cease speaking. He sounded like a dog.

The Kapo said, "I'm just kidding you, it's not hot at all."

Mirko remained still.

"In fact, it is cold today, again. Like it has been every day for a month now." The Kapo made an exaggerated shiver that produced the sound of friction from the collision of his skin and the blazer. Mirko spun around deliberately.

"Be quiet."

He then turned around again and began shifting his weight. He guessed at how much longer the Commander would be before roll call would begin. He estimated forty minutes.

"Do you know what I used to do to keep my hands warm, you know, before, well, all of this?" In saying so he looked to his left and his right, to indicate all that was around him, but Mirko was facing the other way, his rifle leaned up against his shoulder, and did not see the gesture. Instead, he grunted the same grunt. He didn't know exactly what to do to silence the man. In the week since he'd been at the camp, he'd seen other guards reprimand prisoners, but such instances brought nausea deep into Mirko's stomach. Eventually, he would have to show his ruthlessness. Or, more precisely, develop it. Mirko prepared himself for this first experience; the Kapo would be the first to recognize Mirko as a great impenetrable wall, over which no insubordination could scale.

The Kapo continued, "I would warm my hands on the open flame of my stovetops. It sounds genius, I know. But sometimes, if my mind was absently wandering, my hands would lower just that one millimeter enough to catch my knuckle hairs on fire. Sometimes I wouldn't know until the smell."

All of it disgusted him. The subtlety, the brilliance, the single proponents of the one grand organism that worked mechanically to deny the existence of a considered national burden. Something about it reminded Mirko of his childhood, but most of that was so shrouded in the falsity of memory that it seemed a pleasant dream awakened from and disappointed at because of its fantasy. Where Mirko stood brought him the most sinister feeling of personal filth. He knew there was a punishment awaiting him, but stood where he was anyway.

When he first met the Commander, he was told to put his ear to a furniture truck, to listen for movement. Or, more appropriately, no movement. The next time they met, the Commander gave him advice in the small quarters of his personal office, where he interviewed each of his new guards.

"What is your name again?"

"Mirko, Sir."

"Mirko what, soldier?"

"Erinnerung, Sir. Mirko Erinnerung."

"Yes. Sit down."

Mirko had been standing in the taught taut posture of a German soldier. He sat immediately, perhaps too quickly, across from the Commander at his desk.

"Do you know why you're here, Mirko?"

"To serve Germany."

"No. Not why they tell you you're here. Not how you're supposed to respond. But why you're really here, Mirko."

"Sir?"

"Do you know why you were sent to me? To this camp?"

"No, Sir." Mirko felt uncomfortable sitting down across from the Commander. It was too informal, too much like a casual meeting at a café. He half expected a waiter to appear for their drink order.

"You're here to replace a soldier who lost his footing near the wire."

Mirko said nothing. He did not make eye contact with the Commander but focused on the middle of his desk. The Commander put his hand, palm up, on the desk where Mirko was looking.

"What are you looking at?"

"Sir?"

"What are you looking at?"

"Nothing, Sir." Mirko hated being in the room with the Commander. He was frightened of the man, of the situation, of his reputation. The way the other soldiers spoke of his superficial kindness in lieu of a deeper ruthlessness.

"I am not as cruel as they say. You can look at me." Mirko did not look up at the Commander. "Erinnerung, look at me." He did as he was told. This was the first moment that he knew how the camp worked. Not even being there a full day, he knew it was through this sort of intimidation that the organism lived on. And like the Permanents, who also knew the game of fear, he was helpless against it.

"What do they call you where you are from?"

"Mirko."

"No. As a child. What did they call you when you were a child?" The Commander's large smile inflated into caricature.

"They called me Mirko."

"No." The Commander's head slumped quickly to the table and knocked the wood loudly and violently, then sprang up in recoil. Mirko winced at the loud thump. "Surely there was another name. A pet name. Nickname. What was it?" The flush red mark on the Commander's forehead expanded out like a puddle and Mirko glanced at it. The Commander pointed with two fingers at his own eyes; Mirko returned his own eyes to look at them.

Mirko thought for a moment. His desire to please was level with his anxiety to do the same. Suddenly, it came to him. "Miracle," he said in one sonorous burst. Three syllables from another language that made him immediately think back to Gregor taunting him. The memory usually made him upset; now, it warmed him to think of his brother. "Mirko the Miracle."

"Miracle. English, eh? Yes, I see. Listen to me, Mirko. There is something very important that I need to tell you, something that will make your survival in this place easier. Because Mirko, this is a bad place. You know that. It's in your eyes just as sure as it is in your heart. This is a bad place, and I know it too. But of course *good* and *bad* have always been a matter of perspective. But this place will swallow you, and for the rest of your life you will be digested by it, unless you hear me now."

Mirko continued to look at the Commander, though it caused him great displeasure.

"I know it, too," the Commander said, as if in a moment of clarity. Mirko, however, felt the words in deep obscurity.

The Commander continued, "When you walk out there, in charge of the Permanents, when you see what you will see, remember that the direst lesson to learn is to be content with one's place. You. Them. Both. Content with one's place. In the large sense, your country. In the small sense, your home. In the largest sense, your reality. In the smallest sense, yourself."

Mirko thought of his country, home, reality, and self. Their definitions were not congruent with the words the Commander spoke quickly at the end of his lecture. They were rushed, tried and tired after multiple deliverances to all the incoming guards. The concepts of country, home, reality, and self metamorphosed into bastardized versions of value. It was as if the Commander was reading from a script and something about that took some of his power away. It was a moment when fraudulence attempted to wallow behind confidence. It was all very sad.

The Commander finished briskly, "Learn this and you won't be digested. You'll be shit out whole, or at least the closest semblance of whole. Now leave."

Mirko got up and made to leave.

"Oh, and Mirko."

He turned, regarding the wood at the center of the Commander's desk again.

The Commander whistled two notes, one in and one out, "Eyes, Mirko."

Mirko looked up at the Commander's eyes.

"Mind the wires."

In line, the Kapo stepped a bit closer to Mirko and leaned in to whisper in his ear a second time, "You are no man." Mirko's heart froze like his body. "I've seen them and you're not one of them."

Mirko justified himself by pretending to practice patience. But really, he was afraid, more afraid than ever before in his life. More than on the dangerous grounds of the Zwinger with the greedy fingers of the needy; more than at the admonishments of Gregor. More than even amongst the machinery of the cigarette factory, with its metal animal sounds. Then, Mirko had the arms of his city to hold him. Here, what the Kapo said scared him so totally, that he shook inside of his uniform, tiny imperceptible quivers that were perhaps in his blood, tripping along the veins. He was scared because he had to act; he was scared because it was most likely true.

He turned to face the Kapo, knowing that he would have to grip his rifle at its passive end and point it with the destructive end at the man and force him to back down. He did not, however. It remained on his shoulder, fixed and bouncing with the trembles. The Kapo was so much smaller than Mirko that their confrontation seemed almost comical. Mirko's thick-soled boots and the Kapo's oversized blazer produced delusions of grandeur and inconsequence—respectively—for their contest. The jovial nature of the Kapo's earlier comments was snuffed out in the stoic stare he placed upon Mirko's eyes. Two dogs growling.

"I will pretend you've said nothing and it will be the last time I pretend such a thing," said Mirko.

"You are not a man." The Kapo's words were spoken so slowly that there seemed a pause between each.

"Fall back into line now."

"Have you seen a man?"

"Now, Kapo."

"They do not look like you. That is all I mean. Men look different."

Mirko unshouldered his rifle and pointed it limply at the Kapo's chest and said, "I will not give you another chance. I will shoot you."

"I know you will," the Kapo said.

Mirko raised his aim from the Kapo's chest to his face.

"None of you are men. You are the vermin you pretend to eliminate."

Mirko's breaths raised and lowered the rifle a centimeter up and down. His finger put its first pressure on the trigger.

"You are a rat. And a rat cannot kill a man."

By then, the scene had caused a commotion amongst the other prisoners and guards. No one moved, but all watched. This was a moment of balance, and Mirko knew it. He felt the eyes of hundreds fixed to his back as they watched eagerly for the outcome. The other guards judging the new recruit, the other prisoners awaiting the all-too-common end to the insubordination. The words of the Commander returned to Mirko's head. *Content with one's place.* He would have to react in seconds; the moment did not call for deliberation. His training was strict and purposeful: end any enmity immediately. Mirko took the few seconds to consider his place and the amount of his contentment with it; what he found was that he was not content at all. The brilliant organism that was this place, though it amazed him, did not bring him anything worth considering joy. It was digesting him.

The Kapo said slowly, "A rat can kill a man but it cannot kill what is in a man."

It was suicide, death by insubordination; the Kapo had reached his final breaking point, the limit all men have. The guards would talk about it over card games or on duty late: the Permanents who ran for the fences, flinging themselves upon them as if falling into bed. They swore there was a moment of serenity in their faces, as slowly, they glided through the air, diving forward so their front would hit first, as if they intended for their last vision to be the grounds outside, where deer often pranced. The guards would talk of taking shots at the men, to kill them with bullets before they died on the wires, to deny them the last satisfaction that their death was their own.

Mirko thought of the Frauenkirche and the Neumarkt cobbles around it, and whispered, "Please."

Whispered, almost below the level of hearing, a plea.

The Kapo looked back at him, a world of understanding in a word, and fell back in line.

CHAPTER 12

"**D**id you have any friends then?"

I was considering New Orleans as a southern place when he asked me the question I wasn't expecting. Miami is further south, but it is not southern. This place is. People's mannerisms are more pronounced here, carnival big like they are constantly stage acting. Around me is a constant action, and South looks as uncomfortable as I feel. This is the first time South is in the South. He takes advantage of the open container laws; in his hand is a beer in a plastic cup larger than his hand, which I thought would have been impossible, given its impressive size. He takes small sips as if from warm coffee and follows me around the points stationed along the ground of the memorial, which present us with different designs on long black pillars that are supposed to represent concepts of what we pretend we aren't thinking of when we're not talking: those times between South's staunch social observations when a morose silence between us suggests we're thinking about the same thing. We always are, by the way.

Thinking the same thing.

My story.

The tale infused in the silence between us. Sunken grey faded words to match the numbers I carry with me that aren't mine. I've survived nothing.

Did I have any friends then? I did.

"It's the yellow star, yeah? They're sure obsessed with putting that son of a bitch in every memorial, like you want to see that everywhere, right?"

I think to myself: at least it's not bronze bodies twisted into grotesque shapes. A flame. A hand. But I nod. The black pillars of New Orleans's version of memory come together with yellow designs on each to make the star when you stand at the memorial's suggested spot while looking. "Clever, I guess," South says.

"I had a friend," I say. This is more provocative a response than I've ever given South.

"He died, yeah?"

"Yeah, Lombard. He died."

"I'm sorry. No, I mean I'm really sorry. You want to tell me about him?"

How do I tell my new friend about my old friend? About the young man that got me through those days. The ghost breathes into me suddenly. The origins of the word *please*. The muscles of my stomach constrict upon themselves and I double over, right there on the concrete of the memorial. South is on a knee at my side instantly, trying to help me up though I want to be down on the ground. I want to be in it. People visiting the same memorial look at South and me, on the concrete.

"I see his face," I say.

"Don't talk about it. You don't have to."

"I killed him."

South doesn't hesitate. "No you didn't Old Man, you didn't kill anyone." I nod at South, penitent, but he shakes his head negative more fiercely.

By now some of the onlookers come over to ask if I'm okay. They presume I'm having a heart attack. It's exciting, the prospect of watching someone die. South waves them off.

"I'm sorry," I say.

"Knock it off Old Man, it's a sorry business. Let's get a Po Boy."

I let him pull me up. The others move off into their lives. The drama is over; the histrionic old man has returned to his senses, has come back to the world of appetites and frailties.

I move slowly, and South does his best to be patient with me, though I see in the way he takes quick steps back and forth between me and our destinations that I'm holding him up. This could be at as insignificant a stop as a restroom or as enormous as a new skyline. Of the latter, one is succeeded by the next, seemingly more grandiose, always trumping the one before, a contest of height. Each new city seems to me like a whole new country, full of different customs and attitudes and speed. The truth is, I sleep through the majority of the driving, waking only when the violent tumbling of the rumble strips in the shoulder sound angrily at South for nodding off. His immediate reaction is to pretend that nothing is wrong, that he didn't nearly just kill us. I'll look at him, drowsy from the passenger seat, and he'll say, "It's what they're there for," meaning the rumble strips. But because I'm almost always asleep, it's as if I am transported from one city to another without consciousness. The feeling is an alarming mixture of dizziness and thrill.

Some Kapos had relationships with the guards. I tell this to South without solicitation, when I wake up after a rumbling. Perhaps I am still half asleep, dreaming the constant dream of beautiful sky and grazing deer and everything else. He doesn't know what a Kapo is, so I tell him.

"I'd look it up, but my hands are full." He nods once to each hand on the steering wheel, fastened to the appropriate numbers of an analog clock, and I smile.

This is a peace offering, in a sense. This small mote of information, a portion of the potion. My memory vivisected by cowardice and urgency. South does all the driving; this is me pulling my weight.

I tell him that some guards had no real concept of the politics of the war. That some had no sinister interest in the Permanents, but that they were following orders. There were God-terms thrown around, camp jargon you'd hear guards discussing while waiting for roll call or on long marches. Treaty of Versailles. Final Solution. This type of guard would often talk long with the Kapos. Mostly, the conversations centered on common things far removed from the war: their hometowns, their children, what their mother cooked that couldn't be replicated. You have to remember that in a sense, the soldiers were prisoners too.

"Bullshit," South speaks under his breath but loud enough to have his objection noted, his eager anger the commonplace response to the accepted symbol of everything evil. This was how they taught it in schools, in textbooks: you were instructed about how one must project their anger. History was rote emotion.

Most didn't want to be there. You can't blame them for that. Perhaps you can blame them for taking out their aggression on the Permanents, or that they followed so blindly what was so obvious a contradiction to their own humanity, but you cannot fault them for being there. They never wanted to be in a place like that. No one did. No one could.

South stared out the windshield and turned on the windshield wipers when it rained. He turned them off when it stopped. I could tell it made him angry, what I said about not blaming the soldiers. He thinks I have Stockholm Syndrome or something. I don't wish to make him feel that way, but I suppose he has just as much a right to be angry as I do for feeling guilty. People's emotions are justified always in that they are feeling them.

I continue, because I'm fully awake now and giving South what he deserves, the truth for once. I tell him that the Kapos and guards mostly talked about common things, but on occasion, they would venture into the philosophical discourse of trying to figure out the war and how it came to be that there was a divide and that the Permanents and guards were on contrasting sides of the divide. Hitler was a hero to the guards. A means to national salvation. Because one war caused the next and will cause the next forever. I tell South, if you're not careful with something, it will break. And sometimes broken things have sharp edges. South doesn't have a lot of time for figurative language. He looks uneasily into the rearview.

I tell him, "Basically. If you try to kill something, it will try to kill you back."

This, he understands.

When we stopped at a diner a half hour before, South asked me which country I had originally come from. He said it just like that, originally come from, as if I was packaged and shipped away.

"Germany."

"Germany?"

"Germany."

He assumed I was from Israel or something. His puppy-ignorance, charming.

"They did that to their own people?"

"Yes."

South thumbed the bun of a cheeseburger that looked like every cheeseburger out on the road. The superfluous ketchup leaked out of the back and left a red puddle that grew every time he lifted the burger for a bite. "But really," I said, sitting next to him with a black decaffeinated coffee and a slice of pumpkin pie, uneaten, on the bar in front of me, "we're all our own people."

Back in the car, I tell South that the guards were children. The Permanents were almost all older than the guards. His eyebrows raise, this is new information for him, but he doesn't question it so I suppose it makes sense.

We didn't end up getting a Po Boy. Well, not immediately. Instead, we walked the small distance to the famed Mississippi River and sat down to watch it. Across the water was Algiers, and an enormous bridge that brought Algiers to New Orleans stood proudly to our right. Ferry boats sounded steam horns that called along the coast and South and I stared into the brown water. It smelled as all rivers do, a little rancid but of life. Its movements were lively, the waves majestic, the precise original of countless replicas. The Mississippi River. One of the things in the world that endlessly shouts how beautiful the world is. *Take me as an example*, it says. Which I try to.

"*I* actually did kill someone," South said there, on the banks of the Mississippi.

I looked at him questioningly.

He was crying. A subtle cry, a masculine cry. He was staring into the water as he had been before, but tears came at their own accord, not changing his tone or breaking his voice. He did not weep; he simply did not prevent his eyes from watering. This was the Mississippi's doing.

I tried him, "Lombard?" He didn't respond, but drew air simply because it was there to draw.

"No but I mean it, Old Man, yeah? I really did kill someone. In Philadelphia. I wanted to tell you, before." He watched a piece of driftwood pass us and move on until it was out of sight. The riverboats went back to their docks, exchanged people, and set off again. "It's why I moved to D.C."

Behind us, the memorial's black pillars made an obscure design that I didn't understand, regardless of the artist's assertion that the image represented the heroism of prisoners. I then understood that a hero was someone who took something broken and used the sharp edges to make you think there was no danger in risking being cut.

CHAPTER 13

"Please, I cannot know your name," Mirko said to the Kapo. "Let me continue to call you 'Kapo.' I cannot bear to have your name with me if something happens to you."

"If? Perhaps *when* something happens to me. This is more appropriate. And what if something happens to you? I know *your* name, yes? Mirko the Miracle. And how am I to live with that knowledge, Mr. Miracle? Every day with your name and your face, with me always. No."

"It's different."

"I see no difference."

"It is, Kapo."

"You see there. That is not my name. You speak to me closely and yet you call me by a name that is not my own. Like these numbers." He showed Mirko his arm, "These, too, are not my own. But you guards like to give us things that aren't ours while taking away all of the things we want."

"That is not fair."

"You're right. It is not." The two men smiled in the darkness just outside of the bunker. They sat upon two empty tin cans that once held coffee and smoked cigarettes from Mirko's ration.

"I treat you meanly," the Kapo said, "but you are right. Perhaps we should call this illusion what it is."

"What is it?"

The Kapo took a long draft from the cigarette and exhaled the smoke contentedly. "Late night academic discourse." They laughed quietly.

"Don't you need sleep?"

"Do you?" the Kapo responded.

"Kapo."

"Yes? Well, don't you?"

"But I am supposed to be awake now."

"And me, when am I supposed to be awake? When you tell me? Please let me have the one thing I can control, my own sleep."

"Fair."

"Still," he said, looking around to the extent that he could see his surroundings, "I get a lot from this."

"Yes? What?"

"Mirko, please."

"Okay yes. But it's a terrible way to spend your time."

"Would you rather I go into my bunk and sleep, leave you alone to guard me all night? I mean, figure it this way. If I keep awake, I'll keep you awake, and you can guard me so much more easily."

"I don't follow."

"If I go sleep, perhaps you will be envious of my sleep and will perhaps fall into sleep yourself. Then I will escape, which will be very bad for you. Which, then, would be very bad for me, because I know your name and would have to live forever knowing the name of the man I killed."

"I see." Mirko leaned back on his coffee can against the wall of the bunker. "Is it true what you said, about the burners on your stove?"

"The what?"

"The burners, Kapo."

"I still cannot get used to you calling me that. It would be like my saying to you, *soldier*."

"I am often called *soldier*."

"By your friends?"

"Is that what we are?"

"How else can it be defined?"

"But I am here to guard you. To keep you in line."

"And for me, I keep you in line. Without me, you would have nothing to guard. It's all words, Mirko. Just like our names. I'll shut up about it. But I do want you to know my name. I will tell you one day."

"Ok. It is agreed. One day I will know your name. Now, about the burners."

"In my apartment?"

"Yes. Did you really warm your hands on the flame that came from your stovetop?"

"Surely you know how cold it can be, in the winter in Germany. The kind of cold that makes gloves useless in warming your fingers. Yes. I used the stove."

"It seems a desperate thing to do."

"Not all Jews are rich. That is something the Reich is increasingly mistaken about."

Mirko crushed the finished cigarette into the ground below his boot. He had been on duty in the evenings every day for the past month. There was supposed to be a rotation; it was believed that seeing the sun was integral to the psychological well-being of the guards. But he was new, and moreover, distant in some way from the other guards, so it turned out that his rotation on the overnight shift lasted much longer than the others.

"Where are you from?" Mirko asked.

"I'm from where you're from."

"We are both German, yes. But where?"

"Saxony."

"Yes?! As am I! Where from?"

"Shhh. Mirko. Keep your voice down. We wouldn't want to wake the prisoners."

"The Permanents."

"Yes. The Permanents. You guards are sick with the way you name things."

"Please stop including me with them."

“What? You are suddenly not a guard?”

“No, I am not.”

“No. You are not. That is good.”

“So where are you from in Saxony?” Mirko asked again.

“You tell me first, where are you from?”

“Dresden.”

“And so am I.”

“No,” Mirko exclaimed with surprise.

“Indeed. Our Florence on the Elbe. I am.”

“But I didn’t know you.”

“Nor I you, and are you no less from Dresden?”

“But don’t you think we would have seen each other?”

“Perhaps we have. Have you any idea how many people live in Dresden?” the Kapo asked.

“Why are you not as surprised by this as I am?”

“Why? I don’t know. Dresden is just a place.”

“Then you are not from Dresden.”

“No?”

“If you were, you would know it to be more than just a place.”

“All places are just places.”

“No. Dresden is different.”

“In what way?”

“I don’t know.”

“You’ll have to figure out a different argument.”

Mirko reached to the ground behind him and pulled up a canvas bag. From it, he took two loaves of bread, three apples, a handful of figs, and five small stalks of sugar cane, which he handed awkwardly to the Kapo.

“The apples are overripe,” said the Kapo.

“Would you like me to take them back?”

The Kapo inspected the food and chuckled to himself, “It’s nice doing business with you.”

The Kapo got up from his can and entered the bunker. Mirko could hear whispers from the inside. They sounded like muted glee, as if an effort was made to suppress any elation felt by the Permanents who participated in Mirko's clandestine offerings. Not a single one of them ever thanked him, as it was agreed upon by Mirko and the Kapo; any outward sign of affection might reveal what was happening, and would surely result in mortal retribution. Instead, they made eye contact with their guard, knowing glances, then averted their eyes, and were not appalled when Mirko would mock beat the Kapo with the end of his gun or boot, a brutal showmanship acted out in propriety. Insipid status quo. The functions of normalcy. To keep the hounds off their scent.

The agreement was simple but never spoken exactly: Mirko would provide the Permanents of the Kapo's bunker with whatever extra food he could find. He would meet the Kapo one night a week outside, in the very corner of the camp, where the two wire fences met; there, in the shadow of the Kapo's bunker, Mirko would hand over the food. It was his idea, and immediately, the Kapo rejected it.

"You will be killed."

"So will you. Then we agree, it is both our risk."

The Kapo thought about it in the silence presented by the final absence of the last whisper. "Why?"

"I don't know, Kapo. Maybe because I cannot sleep."

"You cannot sleep?"

"No."

"Why did you become a soldier?"

"Because I had to."

"You did not have to."

"But I did. And you would have done the same. To see your own sister starving. You would have done the same?"

"But all this." The Kapo's gesture included everything. "You joined for this?"

"I didn't know."

"Of course you didn't. And now you cannot sleep." The Kapo's voice was rich with theatrical pity.

Mirko stood taller than the man but felt shorter. "This is all I can do."

And the Kapo said, "Okay."

At first, the exchanges went quickly and quietly. The two would meet, and Mirko would hand the extra provisions off to the Kapo, who would return quietly to the bunker and share what he obtained. It was usually rotting vegetables or fruits, on occasion breads, and once, meat. Mirko would steal from the guards' mess hall, or from an incoming shipment, whenever possible. He was careful and fast. He was never noticed.

One evening, as the Kapo was walking away from Mirko, he stopped and turned around.

"What about the others?"

"The others?"

"The other bunkers. Are you feeding them, too?"

"No. Just yours."

"Why mine?"

"Because I had to choose. That is why. I can get enough for one bunker, and I had to choose."

"Then why choose mine?"

"I don't know. It's not as if I gave it a lot of thought, Kapo."

"I notice this place is run with a lot of random choosing."

"It is," Mirko said. "And I chose your bunker. Do you want me to choose another instead?" Mirko was even more exhausted than when he first arrived, and he felt lonely and abandoned when the Kapo did not return his gifts with the affection and appreciation for which he'd hoped. What is true is that Mirko felt empty for *being* at the camp, for being there and being part of its construction. He was able to comprehend his place in the history of the camp, and knew that from the future, his actions there would be condemned, and that he would have to be punished. His only personal recourse was to do whatever he could to help the Permanents. He knew that the help was barely plenty. Enough to make survival more possible but still pitiful in its effectiveness. But it was all he could do, considering everything. To him, it was a pittance and a penance, a small offering of sorrow to keep himself alive. The gesture was as selfish as it was selfless. And Mirko wanted the Kapo to commend him for his bravery and sacrifice. For his hospitality. For his empathy. For the salvation he provided in a little canvas sack. But Mirko had received no such gratitude and it bothered him. It bothered him mostly because he knew he did not deserve it anyway.

The Kapo looked at what Mirko had just given him then looked around at all the other bunkers. Darkness surrounded them but the wood that made their walls was illuminated in the bright floodlights that covered the grounds in a sheet of white. He said, "Okay," and took the food back into his bunker.

Eavesdropping on Mirko and the Kapo on the evenings they met would give the impression that the two were fast friends, sitting at a café in a city with wide boulevards, old men recalling the lives they used to live. To a blind man, it would seem they were living out their days under a nostalgic, quiet comprehension of their simultaneous histories with amiable brotherhood. But only to a blind man. To those who could see, Mirko and the Kapo would be sitting in the shadow of a wooden bunker where inside, four-hundred men would be waiting for the conversation's end so they could split between them a few rotting apples. They would lie on the planks of their wooden bunks and strain to hear the whispers—they often thought they heard laughing—and wait for the door to open and their Kapo to return. Some Kapos, they knew from observation, were so in league with the guards that they exhibited a congruent cruelty with their captors. Those Kapos were known to physically assault their Permanents, or condemn them by exposing their transgressions to the guards, to sneer at their men as if they themselves were part of the camp's fluid functionality. The Permanents of Mirko's Kapo, then, were appreciative of the small man in charge of them, and forgave the entertainment he received from his liaisons with the German guard that one night a week.

Their relationship did not flourish immediately. During the day, the Kapo stood with his grey blazer until the weather warmed enough that it was not needed. When Mirko was on duty during the day, he would look over at the man, as inconspicuously as possible, and, noting how thin and vacuous he looked without his coat, tried to exchange a knowing glance. The Kapo wouldn't return Mirko's look. He did not want Mirko to feel like a savior in the camp. Mirko needed that, needed to feel that he was of the ruling party, but was an insurgent, a valiant hero amidst a sea of treacherous indecency. Mirko wanted to represent humanity, where humanity was showing its most filthy side, and he did it through piecemeal peace offerings that would scream rejection through the future tomes of history. The Kapo wanted nothing of his salvation. He valued what was given him, indeed, and he knew the extreme risk the guard was taking, but he also knew the object was selfish; Mirko was providing for him and the Permanents of his bunker simply because it relinquished him of his own burden. Because, the Kapo thought, no man could ever be in league with such an event without understanding the jeopardy of his self. There was no excuse justified enough, no reparations valuable enough, no rotten apples nourishing enough that would ever relinquish one's collusion with evil.

The Kapo refused to lighten Mirko's load by taking upon himself, more weight.

Mirko had arms and legs. He had a head that held a brain. He had skin and blood and inside he had organs that, in conjunction, performed the perfunctory performances to keep him alive. In his chest, he had a heart. But no matter any of the evidence that would testify to Mirko's humanity, he still held his ear against the cargo box of furniture trucks. He still fired absently into the dark on attempted escapes. He still wore his colors.

Despite the Kapo's attitude toward Mirko, the Permanents of his bunker viewed Mirko as a sympathizer. They whispered to each other when out of earshot about the brave German soldier who condemned the camp and who brought them stolen food. The Kapo overheard such conversations and pleaded for his Permanents to cease discussing the situation. He knew that if word got out beyond his bunker to the other Permanents of the camp, there could be significant repercussions. When one group is in want and another is in have, the resulting hunger can become savage.

But no matter how snidely the Kapo treated Mirko throughout the weeks that became months outside of the bunker, in the shadows made by the floodlights, Mirko was still there, every time. The Kapo couldn't keep completely angry at the soldier, who was as young as he was, vulnerable in the dark despite the rifle still at his side, who yearned to suggest his place outside of this place. There was something to be said at least for this, Mirko's desire to separate himself from his kinsmen. It was not absolution to the Kapo, but it was a brief sabbatical from the standard plain hatred he maintained for his captors.

It struck him suddenly. I hate him hates me hates he hates we. He felt as barbarous as the soldiers themselves.

"Both of us are German, you know," he said to Mirko upon being handed one week's food ration. Mirko had absently handed the Kapo the food and was turning to return to his post when this first bit of conversational pleasantry was offered. Between the men were the stillness of night and the blackness of it. The floodlights hummed like giant insects, the noise equally as displeasing to sleepers as the light. But between them was something else as well. A distance, a gap. An echoless canyon traversed by no bridge. The Kapo intended the comment to be conversational, somewhat friendly, to show a bit of allegiance in the decency explored by the guard, but as it left his mouth, it was filled with the same contempt as all of the words he'd spoken to Mirko.

Mirko didn't know at first how to respond. He didn't so much hear what the Kapo said in favor of the fact that the Kapo had said anything at all. He stood there looking into the direction that he estimated the Kapo's eyes to most likely be, though all that was there was the black outlined silhouette of a human being.

"You are not talking," the Kapo said.

"Is it a requisite?"

"Both of us," the Kapo repeated, "are from the same country. Germany. We are countrymen."

"Yes."

"Yes. It is true. We speak our language don't we?"

"Yes."

"You are much for words tonight," the Kapo said sarcastically.

"As are you," Mirko said literally.

The Kapo looked at Mirko's black silhouette as well. Two men standing and looking at each other's shadows.

"Thank you."

Mirko tilted his head in confusion. It was the first time he had heard those words in so long. "For what?"

The Kapo laughed and held up his hands, "Well, these."

Mirko lowered his head, "Yes."

The Kapo waited silently for Mirko to say something, but he stood there shifting his weight from foot to foot, the way he did his first day at the camp, that uncomfortable volley back and forth that made him look like a tilting tower in the wind.

"So we are both from Germany," the Kapo repeated.

"We are."

"So we are brothers."

Mirko looked up at the man, but still, his face was nothing in the night. "We are brothers?"

"Yes."

"Okay, yes."

"Considering everything."

They were adversaries pitted against one another endlessly in the spinning mechanism of the organism consuming and digesting around them; Mirko and the Kapo, at that moment, for the moment, became what was foreign to them both: neighbors of the same land, of different blood, in a common accident of humanity and history.

Mirko and the Kapo sat smoking cigarettes from the former's ration.

"You know, I never smoked one of these before I came here."

"A cigarette?" the Kapo asked, partly surprised. He reclined next to Mirko against the bunker wall and tried to blow the smoke away from the building so that the other Permanents wouldn't smell the smoke and salivate for the taste. "Never one?"

"No. It was always the way men coughed who smoked them. I never understood the desire to smoke these, that just made you cough like that."

"But they can be so sweet, yes? The smoke of it, in and out. Proof that you are breathing. Your breath made visible."

"Maybe. I mean yes. I understand."

Between them was the obligatory satchel of food, but it went unnoticed, as it had then for the last few months of their secret meetings, at least for an hour or so while the men sat and spoke of the most trivial important things they could think of.

The Kapo inhaled and exhaled, blowing the smoke away, angling the line away from the floodlights. "To smoke. This truly is the luxury. Though it is making my marches difficult."

At every mention of the hardships the Kapo went through, Mirko felt another sickening jolt of shame.

"Kapo."

"I'm sorry to mention it, Mirko."

"No. What else can I do?"

"What else? What can you do? Else? As if there was something you could do in the first place. Look around you, Mirko; this place is bigger than you. It's bigger than this place, even. We have no idea how big any of it truly is. How are you to challenge something the size of which you can't even fathom?"

"It *is* big."

"It *is*. And we are small inside of it. Insects that can't even comprehend the larger reality of it."

"What larger reality?"

"I don't know, Mirko. I just said I couldn't comprehend it."

"Try."

"Try to understand the impossible? That would take an arrogance I've lost since coming here."

Mirko took a shallow drag on the cigarette. Any deep breath and it would cause him to cough. In the camp, a cough could be fatal not in its implication, but in its sound. He looked beyond the fences, into the evening that got darker the further away from them that it went. From blue to black to nothing. It was paradise, considering.

"I suppose," the Kapo continued, "we are simply to live in the place we find ourselves."

"Even here?"

"Even here."

The line reminded him of the Commander's early advice, which displeased him in how opposing forces played by the same rules. Mirko, finished, held the cigarette up between his forefinger and thumb and showed it to the Kapo. "Kapo, did I ever tell you about my brother Gregor?"

"No. I know of your sister, but you've never once mentioned a brother."

The lit tobacco at the end of Mirko's cigarette burned the butt as the cigarette was spent, but Mirko kept it held up to make orange faces of himself and the Kapo. "He worked in a cigarette factory in Dresden between the wars."

"I know of them. There were many."

CHAPTER 14

It was dawn in the miraculous sense that there was an absolute silence in the streets. People coveted the final minutes before the sun's rising, they envied those who had extra minutes in bed, so they stayed in theirs for as long as possible. Every morning, every city became a ghost town. The sky unperceivably lightened a shade at a time, from high darkness, in hues in the spectrum of blue, today: bright, clear, and open. The genesis of changing sky acted to awaken the buildings of Dresden, themselves seeming to stretch at the suggestion of a new day, reveal themselves alert and yawning, back into the world. The emptiness of Altstadt was so complete that the smallest footfall produced a noticeable echo. Mirko's small steps clapped loudly on the cobbles; his direction: the factory.

The further into his journey Mirko went, the more he was able to see the streets present themselves in the morning light. At first, everything was black and infinite in its darkness. Soon after, the shadows of structures made themselves present; and a bit later, the beginnings of sun brought the world into sight, the old structures of the city once again in the view of day, content in the consistency of orbits and solar revolutions and slumbers and waking. It was a cycle of two parts, the waking day and the sleeping night. A ballet. In existence only because their opposite existed. In this sense, death explains what there is to life.

The light developed and the shape of things shifted, but Mirko could have run the route blindfolded. The swiftest course was plotted deep into the map of his mind; his knowledge of Dresden's streets complete as if he'd laid the foundation himself, as if he were its proud architect. His shoes were beginning to come apart at their seams, crevasses widening where thread was weakening. He could feel the cold air on his feet inside the shoes. He could feel the cold air everywhere. In his haste to leave the house, he did not put on a coat or hat. Adette yelled after him to dress properly for the weather but managed only to secure a scarf around his neck before he was out of the door in a flash of wind. She thought of him, blazing through the streets, a blotch of color, like something moving in a photograph. He reminded her of Gregor when he was younger, a thought that caused her to stall. Mirko had the same sort of haste laced within him; it was a part of him to move, a part Gregor tried valiantly to ignore but Mirko rode with child-ish glee. Adette loved Mirko so completely when she real-ized how much he reminded her of Gregor, who she loved so much. Her brothers were her life, and they were similar in that they were made of the same stuff, perhaps an en-ergy that made stillness impossible. To Adette, Mirko was a peaceful and ignorant boy, able to only see the world as he decided to see it. She envied him of his perspective.

Behind him, the arms of his scarf clapped their fringed hands.

Adette and Mirko had fallen asleep the night before on the floor next to the fireplace, waiting for Gregor to return home from work. He had left upon hearing of Mirko's en-counter with the foreman and did not return that evening.

When Mirko and Adette had awoken in the morning, Gregor was still not home.

Adette sent Mirko immediately.

The walls of the factory met Mirko's momentum in a clash of wills. His speed was renowned in the town and the factory's walls were stubbornly steadfast with industry. The collision was catastrophic. Mirko, a boy, stood stock still in front of the factory gate, his feet spread apart and his shoulders square, as if challenging the structure. The colored dome seemed a lung at full inhale and the black smoke spread again from the ornate towers in an obscure spray that denied the day. He left it the day before frightened and now stood there in strong opposition. The factory walls raised before him a fortification, protecting the machines that worked men as much as they were worked by men. Perhaps more. The sheer size of the contest did not intimidate Mirko as he looked up from the cobbles underneath him to the building that took his brother's spirit. He stared at it with a profound hatred, something he had as of yet not identified as his true feelings for the building. It was hatred. A boy's hatred identified for the first time. The rite of passage complete, he was one emotion closer to being a man.

Mirko broke his stasis and began walking up to the front gate. His intention was to enter the building and seek out Gregor. He had not thought of a thorough plan, but he knew he would take his brother from the building and take him home.

There, he would place him on his cot.

Cover him with blankets.

Light the fire.

And feed him tea with honey. Honey that he would find, somehow.

He and Adette would care for Gregor until he was well, and when he was, he would never return to that place; Mirko would defeat the factory by removing his brother from it. This was Mirko's best plan, incomplete but sincere.

Mirko put his palm on the front gate when a nearby deep cough slowed his progress. It was familiar, a bottomless cough from fluid-filled lungs, that rose from a simple baritone to the impossible depth of bass. One jerked cough, followed by a few weaker aftershocks that increased in pitifulness as they released. It was Gregor's sound.

Mirko followed the commotion around the factory wall and saw, as he turned the corner, the figure of his brother sitting with his back against the side wall. One of Gregor's knees was bent up to his chest and the other leg was stretched out. His head was bowed forward and his hat lay on his lap, fallen, not placed there. Each of Gregor's arms were at his sides, the heels of his hands pressed into the corner where the factory's walls met the ground so that when he coughed, he involuntarily pushed with both arms and caused his entire body to jolt up away from the wall and fall back helplessly against it.

Mirko rushed over to Gregor and crouched in front of him.

"Gregor!"

Gregor looked up, and in seeing Mirko, smiled, "Miracle."

"Gregor, what are you doing here?"

"They fired me, Miracle." He rolled his head back and indicated his former place of employment. "They fired me."

"Let's go home, Gregor. Come on now."

"They fired me for not coming in today, Miracle." He smirked while looking at Mirko without looking directly at him; his eyes were unfocused and distant. "What people, people are."

"What?"

"What people, people are."

It was still early morning, and only then did Mirko begin to hear the sounds that indicated the day was underway. Behind him, on the street, people went on their way, regarding them with the simultaneous disdain and pity bestowed upon the roofless unfortunate.

"Miracle, sit," Gregor said.

"No. Gregor. You must get up. We will go home. I will make you tea with honey."

Gregor laughed at the proposition. After everything, his brother thought only of tea and honey. Gregor looked at his brother and was glad for him, glad for the reality that he lived in. One where it was always and only tea and honey. Gregor hoped it would continue to be that way for Mirko, but knew also that soon it would not be.

"Miracle, please sit next to me."

"Gregor, we must. . ."

"Mirko."

The sudden use of his true name stunned Mirko into compliance. He sat next to Gregor against the factory wall but was still turned to him. "Mirko, care for Adette. She is sensible but incapable. Do you remember what she teaches you from the Bible?"

Mirko nodded his head.

"Listen to her. Everything she says is true. Listen to what she reads. But care for her Mirko, she is fragile."

Mirko watched his brother, knowing that the information he was being given was important and that he should take distinct notice of everything that Gregor was saying.

"What people, people are," Gregor said again. "Mirko, listen."

The boy turned to Gregor and put his head down on his shoulder. "That's good, Mirko," Gregor said. "Now listen to me."

Mirko quietly cried. Gregor's coughs bounced Mirko's head from his shoulder, but Mirko replaced it there, after every convulsion. He had never heard Gregor speak this way. It was a song, a sweet bird song that moved with affection from his brother's lips into his chest. It was beauty. A moment of brotherly love shared against a wall so tall that neither would ever grow to see over. Mirko felt Gregor's love then, amidst his coughs, in the sonorous tone of his voice, as Gregor talked of beauty, and prepared him for ugliness. For Mirko, the words were terrifying in their poetry, in their prospect.

"Remember the Frauenkirche," Gregor repeated.

He picked Mirko's head off of his shoulder and forced him to look into his eyes. "Remember the Frauenkirche, yes?"

Mirko nodded.

"Yes, Mirko?"

He nodded again.

"Say it."

"Yes."

"Say it."

"Remember the Frauenkirche." Mirko said the words but they were distorted in his voice. His throat seemed to collapse upon itself as he choked over silent sobs. He made sure not to make any noise.

"Good, Mirko. Miracle. Yes." Gregor put his head back against the wall sleepily. "I must rest. Rest with me, Mirko?"

"Okay, Gregor." He replaced his head on his older brother's shoulder.

A minute passed by and Gregor's breathing started calm but grew troubled and ended with the deep bellow of a cough before returning to calm. "Mirko," he said.

"Yes?"

"One day, soon maybe, Germany will be great again. Mirko, promise me that you will be part of what makes Germany great."

"I promise."

"Never be ashamed of this place. Of Dresden. Our beautiful home. The home our mother loved. Love it with all your heart."

"I promise."

"What people, people are."

"I promise, Gregor." He had no concept that this would be the last conversation he would have with his brother.

They fell asleep. Only Mirko woke.

Gregor was sixteen years old.

In the Otherwise Silence

Chapter 15

"Hemingway was a drunk," the man says in a strong English accent.

"We're all drunks, darling," the woman sitting next to the man, across the table from South and me, says as she spirals the ice around her tumbler, "every last drop of us."

I've never seen a woman drink bourbon before. It is exhilarating. I can tell South is pleased as well. So far on the trip, we haven't run into a lot of other people, so meeting these two at a roadside bar just outside Albuquerque provides us with a much-needed relief from the monotony of one another. "You're so obsessed with Americans who wish they were European, dear."

"No. Simply distressed at Europeans wanting to be American."

South says, "Grass always greener, yeah?"

And they both look at him, amazed. A true specimen of colonization gone wrong. The British still have a tendency to view Americans as runaway children; they want to admonish Americans for leaving the nest but are frightened by their wingspans.

The woman's name is Marjorie, which was difficult to deduce with the thickness of her accent pronouncing it. It was a mix between aristocratic and alcoholic, a slurred articulation of English syllables that screamed intellectualism while tumbling down the stairs. She sounded it out for me, her head slunk a little lower and pushed closer, as if my hearing was going bad, "*Mar. Jor. Ie.*" Then for repetitive effect, "*Mar. Jor. Ie.* You see?"

I saw.

Her husband is Bert, a name that doesn't fit him. He is bald but hopeful; elongated strands of hair from the side of his head arch over his crown giving him the mysticism of an age-defying tactical giant. Every tip of his pint glass loses half of its beer, so he's constantly motioning for the waitress to return and refill it. He's heavy but not drastically overweight. The majority of him is frail thin, save for a spherical stomach that pushes out his yellow and sky-blue checkered button-up. Bert smiles constantly.

They're on a trip from Salisbury, which they indicate is such and such distance from London. Lombard's never been to London. I have, momentarily. It was an intermediary, a stopping point for refugees who were on their way elsewhere. I don't mention this, however.

We came into the bar after checking into a motel across the street. South had driven for the better part of the entire day; stopping seldom, he sped on as if toward a purposeful destination instead of killing time, which is what we were really doing. We traversed Texas widthwise and made it just outside of Albuquerque before South gave in; he did so by saying simply, "I need a beer." I thought he deserved it. I had spent the day marveling at the changing scenery of America. From the industrious and metropolitan north to tropical Florida, across to the swamps of the south and now out across the desert, where abruptly everything became a beautiful nothing: the country was always changing. We drove into the desert as if it was commonplace, but it was no such thing. It was a vast openness that frightened me, though I knew I was safely locked in the moving machine South pushed across the asphalt. America is not one singular thing; it is a composite patched together of many different things. I had known it, I am an avid reader, but I was never able to imagine it the way it presented itself to me. Sudden. Startling. Distant mountains in the background and a sightline that veered off in every direction to eternity. Almost immediately, I felt small: how people feel when they remember the Universe.

We entered through saloon doors just inside a proper glass door and made our way to the bar, where South ordered two beers. I felt like I owed it to him to drink what he had ordered, so I did. The beer was cold and I appreciated it. I appreciated the way it confused my confusion concerning the changing scenery of the country. I wouldn't say the sights perturbed me, but I was somehow unsettled. The next beer made that feeling go away and I was left with a *joie de vivre* that simply accepted it all. I could tell South was tired, but the bar was empty save for Marjorie and Bert, who we had yet to meet, and when Bert came to the bar to order another round— "beer for me please and another of the strong stuff for the missus"—and subsequently started a conversation with us, we both felt compelled to join them at their table.

"What we wanted to do, really, was see the America that Europeans don't normally see, you see?" Marjorie says.

"Right, yes," says Bert, who unabashedly runs his hand up and down his wife's thigh under the table, "Most Europeans fancy New York and California. You're considered adventurous if you go to Chicago. Then, of course, people return to England and say they've seen the Midwest."

"Do they go to Philadelphia?" South asks.

"Pardon?" replies Bert.

"Philly, do Brits go there? That's where I'm from, yeah?"

"Yes, I see. Not really, chap. I mean, sadly, the English feel that city to be distinctly tragic, if you will. Should it make you feel any better, we mainly ignore Boston as well. It comes down to principal, I suppose, though none of us will admit to it."

"I'm hungry," Marjorie interjects, "Do you think they have actual food here?"

"I'll ask if the kitchen is open, dear," Bert says, though he makes no move to. Marjorie lights a cigarette and blows the smoke above her head. It stays there and becomes part of the haze, a grey dunce cap spiking from her head. "But yes, so we came and rented a car and just have been making our way across the country, stopping wherever and really trying to see what most Americans do."

"What they *do*," Marjorie sings. She hits her notes awkwardly, then drowns any pretense with the remainder of her bourbon. "How they *are*." Anthropologists, all travelers.

I don't say much, but it doesn't seem to distract them. South is representative for both of us. "So you get around the country, yeah? See anything good?" He's close to five beers in now and South is feeling loose; I can tell it in his posture. I've seen it a number of times in my apartment. It's always around the fifth.

"Oh, we've seen many things."

"Like?"

"Oh. What then, honey, did we see?"

Marjorie thinks, "A lot of crosses."

"Yes. Crosses. Big ones. Sticking out of the ground there just on the highway. We exited the highway and parked by one. There was a guy in a wheelchair there handing out tracts for fifty cents each. We both bought one. Not that we're religious or anything, but he seemed so sad at the foot of that big cross. In his wheelchair. He was quite old. Pardon my saying so."

This last sentence is directed at me. I nod as if to say, it's fine.

"They're almost frightening," Bert says, "the huge crosses. I don't like it when my supreme deity is screaming for attention." Bert laughs to himself.

"Oh, and we're reading. The greats," Marjorie says.

"Yeah?" South says. "Like books?"

"Of course," Bert says. "Like Hemingway."

"Trust fund babies," Marjorie says. "Paid for all their tabs in Paris. Makes European life a lot more romantic than it really is."

"I hardly think you can call Hemingway one of the trust funders," Bert says. Marjorie rolls her *whatever* eyes.

"I've never read any of his books," South says, almost as if he is embarrassed by it.

"Is that right? I suppose I supposed. . ." Bert stops and mentally goes over the clause of his sentence, feeling it didn't sound right. He shrugs as if he's accepted it, "that all Americans read Hemingway."

"Nope," South says, "You'd probably be surprised at how many don't."

"Right. Well. Right now we're doing the Steinbeck leg. Oklahoma to California. We're going to wine country to taste our own grapes of wrath."

"My husband has always had a sinister analysis of literature, especially when he dilutes it with humor," Marjorie interjects from her head's place on the wood of the table where we'd all thought she had fallen asleep. Neither of us really understands what the couple is talking about in their hurried wordiness, mostly because of their accents, but we are content to be amongst other people. In some sense, sharing a space with these others momentarily pauses our constant self-reflection. Perhaps I've found the fondness of friendship.

The emptiness inside of the bar reflects the openness of the desert outside; only the walls divide here and there into suggestions of place. It's gotten so smoky in the bar with Bert and Marjorie smoking and no ventilation, that it's becoming difficult to see the others at the table. South leans on his elbows, bows to expose the top of his head, and wavers back and forth. Rain has begun to fall; it drums on the roof audibly and hypnotically, a metronome to our rhythm. The mixture of alcohol and stagnant smoke is giving me a stomachache, but I do not want to be the one to break up the party. In all likelihood, South and I will sleep for the majority of the day tomorrow, taking off at early evening, to somewhere west. So we'll have rest. The maps in his car are coming apart despite his care. They are beginning to wear at the folded seams, developing new borders of spaces in the midst of old places. South tried to have me navigate at first but found that I was not fit for the task. I don't know how to read maps and spent most of the time tracing the black lines of imaginary borders that divided the states. I wanted to know who first divvied up the country. Who first began serrating the puzzle pieces into independent places of distinction. Similar lines travel the grounds where I'm from, but I've never seen them. When we cross state lines, South and I have to look for welcome signs, or else we would have never known the difference.

Thank goodness for the black lines of borders.

"So you fellows. You've heard plenty of us and our misadventures, I'm sure. We're a long way from Philadelphia, indeed. How do we find ourselves here?" asks Bert. South raises his head a little. I can tell by the way his eyes are bloodshot that he is drunk. We must look strange to them, a stocky drunk man and his elderly companion. They probably presume we are father and son, driving across country on a road trip to all the baseball stadiums, to patch up years of distance at the end of my life.

South nods over at me and says, "Him."

Marjorie can barely hold her head up, and when she tries to sip the bourbon, her shifting hand makes waves in the tumbler which break over the edge of the glass and drip drops on the table. Bert looks over at me confused.

"Him?" he says. It's not exactly the feeling of someone talking about me to someone else while I'm sitting there, but it's like it. I'm a child whose parents are spelling out words across the dinner table so that I can't understand the family's fiscal crisis.

"He's a survivor," South says.

"South," I say.

"He survived the Holocaust."

Both Marjorie and Bert look at me. Remarkably, she is able to keep herself perfectly straight. You would think that the Queen had just walked in. They both straighten up in their chairs, a sign of deserved reference for not dying. The rain picks up; we can hear it falling in tantrums against the roof of the bar, waves crashing our building. It is accompanied by winds that scream eerily as they pass through the emptiness of the desert unimpeded. The walls do not shake and the lights do not flicker, but the bar feels like little sanctity. It feels like, at any point, if it so wanted, the outside could force its way in.

"South," I say again, hoping that the plea in my voice gets him to stop, though I know he is drunk, and there is little likelihood my plea is heard at all. We're all having such a good time; I don't want this to go where it is going. Any pretense of conversation, any travel stories, will be trumped. Suddenly, Bert and Marjorie will go from a British couple on holiday in America, who stop at grandiose crosses and sample Napa wine, to the couple who met a survivor on their journey. It will be the quintessential cocktail hour small-talk conversation starter. *You'll never guess what happened to Marj and me on our trip to the states. We were in this inconspicuous dive bar in...*I will have gone from being a fatherly baseball enthusiast to a hero. Though really, I've survived nothing, and would rather talk about home runs than run home.

"Oh," Bert and Marjorie say in unison. Marjorie continues to say, "How marvelous," but regrets it immediately. She'll chide Bert in the morning for not controlling her ejaculations when she loses her composure.

Bert motions to the waitress and when she walks over, says, "Bourbon. Neat."

"And for you?" she asks, crossing the fifth tally mark through the four vertical soldiers on the bill she's withdrawn from her apron.

"That *is* for me," he responds.

I can tell by the look on her face that Marjorie wants to say something. She looks over to Bert with eyes that carry a message but it goes undelivered. The waitress looks at Marjorie as if to ask if she'll have anything else and by way of response, Marjorie shakes her head quickly, once back and once forth. The waitress glances our way but South and I don't attempt to make eye contact, so she leaves.

"So you're European as well," Bert says. It's meant to be conversational, a change of pace from his wife's random drunk mutterings, but it comes out flat.

"Yes," I say.

"Indeed. Where are you from? I mean originally of course."

"Germany."

Bert lowers his eyes, "I see."

Suddenly I'm a saint born from the land of demons. The histories of our countries sewn into our skins, we are no longer at a bar in New Mexico, we're the sons of our fathers, carrying their weights. South looks over to me as if in an epiphanous moment within his drunkenness. It's a look that says *I'm sorry.* I am not angry with him, however; nor am I angry at Bert or Marjorie, or anyone really. I'm not angry at the thousand things left unsaid, or the thousand things left to fester, wounds becoming the sharp edges of knives that make more wounds. I'm not angry at retribution or reparations. I'm not angry at injustice, as it is not ashamed of itself. I'm not angry at the cyclical mistakes of history, nor forced purposeful ignorance. I'm not angry at hatred, nor am I angry at intolerance. I'm not angry at the villains nor the heroes. The victims nor the abusers. The evil nor the good. I'm not angry at mankind. I'm not angry at the Germans nor the British nor the captors nor the captured. Because all of us at this table are captured in one way or another. By the insignias on our passports or the bodies that hold our souls. We're all stuck; it just so happens to be that we're stuck here together.

No. What I'm angry at are the borders.

It's easy to tell when a man's thoughts are in the unfortunate position of brimming, when they're packed in a cannon with heat behind. South's tells are the slumped shoulders and staring, unblinking eyes. It would be easy to say it was the long drive and the many beers that prompt his confession, but I know it was no such thing; I know because I, too, have a confession, but my thoughts are fastened well, anchored at safe depths. South is too honest to be as fortunate. And when he looks over at me, I know that it is time: South wants to pay his penance.

"You never asked, Old Man, what I did for a living. Why?"

I don't answer because you *don't* answer. One thing I've learned is that there are a number of mythic rules we must abide by, regardless of how we feel about them. South's question is rhetorical because he didn't ask it to me; he asked it to the thoughts bubbling, breaching.

"I was a detective," he says. "Philadelphia Police Department."

Bert and Marjorie have become a British audience, also following mythic proprieties, but only as theatre-goers: they are reverent toward the drama, silent in the dark and prepared to clap in unison at curtain-fall.

"South," I say. It's the only thing I can say. No, there's something else, "Lombard." But neither has an effect. I don't want him to say anymore in front of Bert and Marjorie. He can confess to me because we're in this together. Because I care for him. But they are interlopers here, not in the U.S. but in us, and I want to shield South from how open Truth will make him.

I want all this knowing there is nothing I can do to make it so.

"You never even asked why I was in DC, Old Man, when you knew I was from Philly. Why? Why didn't you care?" He looks up at the wall for a moment, then turns back, "I know why. It's because you knew. Somehow, because of everything that's happened to you, you know these things, yeah? You know a killer because you're a survivor."

"I don't know anything, Lombard."

"And you didn't want to ask because you knew you'd find out what I'd done and then would have to think of me like I know you think of *them*."

"I've survived nothing."

"And I thought I could prove to you that I'm not like them. I'm different because I didn't have any choice. When I met you that day…you remember what I said?"

"You said I'd survived."

"When I saw those numbers, it came to me in a fast pain. It hurt. What happened to you; what I did, I knew it was the same. You take a lot of lives, you take one life."

The rain outside seems to back off; even it wants no part of this.

"So I came up with this idea, yeah? The memorials. I wanted you to see how you, all of you, are remembered. And I wanted you to see that I wasn't like them."

"South," I say. I wish I could be more profound.

"I was a detective. A kid shot a cop, and I found him. I found the kid. I ever tell you I have kids, Old Man? Two of them. They're back in Philly with my wife. Anyway, so

I found the kid who shot the cop, someone I knew. I found him.

"You ever been in one of those neighborhoods, Old Man? You ever see anything like that?"

Marjorie says, "Goodness," and covers her mouth with her left hand. She thumbs her upper lip.

"This is what Americans *do*, Marj," South says. "Trash. Corner bodegas with three-inch plastic shields in front of the cashiers that are so scuffed that you couldn't see through them. Broken sidewalks with weeds coming through the cracks and fat black cockroaches scuffling from shadow to shadow. Multi-colored dime bags discarded like candy wrappers. You know it. It's in every city, the neighborhood everyone avoids but is the one most people know about. Most people think about the city and they think this neighborhood."

South looks up suddenly over at me, "And I'm not saying anything about it, yeah? I'm not passing any judgment on the people who live there or any of that. And I'm not saying anything bad about them. Hell, I've talked to them; I know that they don't want to be there either. A place everyone wants to abandon. We joked, the boys, you know, at the station, about not patrolling there. They used to talk about just letting it be. But it was a joke, because we couldn't.

"Most people are stuck there," South continues. "Permanently there. Ghettos, they call them. Just like where you're from. Ghettos because you're stuck there permanently and no one cares. But in America, we don't kill people with gas; we kill them because we just keep them there and don't let them out. We make animals of men and Holocausts aren't always obvious."

"South," I say. I wish I was more profound because he's become more profound. Or perhaps he's always been, and this is the result of his courage. Maybe, if I had a small portion of what abundance he has, I'd be able to speak as well, to tell my friend just how different he is from the vague *them* he chastises, the evil he mistakes to be so far away: in Germany, sixty years ago. I'm sitting right next to him, and I am absolutely mute. This is what it is to be human, the sinking into solemn hindsight.

"So yeah, Old Man, I was the one who found that kid."

Outside, we are soaked through in moments. It is the kind of rain that walking through feels like swimming through. Parting with Bert and Marjorie, we watch them rush through the rain to their room; we stand there soaking it in. It's useless to rush now. We are saturated.

"I'm sorry," South says.

"For what?"

"For telling them about your numbers."

"It's okay."

Along the line of doors to the various rooms at the roadside motel are flowerpots that attempt to provide momentary beauty from the gravel parking lot to the brown-painted façade of the building. We pass them on the way to our door, small flowers sprouting through the black dirt, a few feet away from the falling rain. They seem to reach as if to drink, but they are under the building's porch overhang, and they are dry. We pass by a pot that has been knocked over in the rain, and, leaning down, South picks it up and rights it, scooping some of the lost dirt from the concrete ground and depositing it back into the pot. Some soil stays with his palm's wetness. He takes the small flowers by their stalks and rights them, so they are all facing up, then proceeds on to our room.

Chapter 16

It had gotten cold again. It was expected, the cold, as it was every year. The dipping temperature of the summer led by degrees into the months of angry cold, cold that whipped the faces of the Permanents and drew tears from their squinting eyes. The length of the marches didn't change when the colds came. There wasn't an abbreviated winter version of the summer journey. The Permanents would still have to move, to walk in semi-straight lines to trenches that seemed always half dug, to trees always half lumbered. To whatever meaningless work they performed for which they had not the slightest concept of productivity. It made a man weary, to work and not know the product he was fashioning. Even the Kapo had lost the glint of his former self, that impossibly sarcastic coyness that prevented Mirko from feeling completely criminal. The months had been difficult for him. Through the last days of summer, the Kapo had taken ill. In the camp, all illnesses were the same, and they were all terminal. The moment a Permanent began feeling ill, the others would move a little further away, keep a bit more distance, avoid direct contact. A cough was akin to a spiraling bullet, working its way in the space of a blink, through the tissues that kept human insides from the outside.

Those who fell ill would often be sent to the infirmary, and would seldom return. The Kapo hid his sickness well, but it spent him, truncating the meetings with Mirko to a few words and the exchange of goods. He would apologize to Mirko, citing his illness as a reason for his shortness. Mirko would wave him off, tell him that he needed his rest, suggest that someone else from the bunker pick up the food. The Kapo had said no, his life was the risk enough. He smiled the lie parents reserve for frightened children. His hand momentarily went up to his head, brushed past the spiraling cowlick, and again said *no*. His hand came to rest on his cheek. His skin tinged soapy-water grey, wrapped so tightly on his figure that Mirko could see his collarbone where the blazer split at his sternum. "One life is the risk enough," he had said. Mirko noted no tone of irony in his voice.

Mirko's worry for the Kapo pervaded his daily work. He carelessly manned his watchtower, the spotlight raking the sky in dense pillars, as he thought of his ill friend. The loudspeakers cackled. The only image in Mirko's mind was the infirmary's door, which showed a man's back but never his front. The Kapo's illness had come so suddenly that it was as good as running for the fences. He knew nothing of medicine, and could not risk being found out to start asking around. The soldiers were just as isolated as the Permanents, on a covert mission that had very little outside intervention. He carried on as usual, as best as he could, supplying the Kapo's bunker with stolen food and waving off his apologies, hoping sincerely and potentially vainly that the Kapo's frail body could fight whatever microscopic villains threatened it.

If the inability for the Kapo to feel relief from his illness was a physical burden, the reclamation of winter's brisk breath was the psychological counterpart. The Kapo woke as the days shortened and joined his marching line at the front, directly behind Mirko, figuring this day or the next would be his final. Each day seemed less likely to lead to a next than the last. The returning cold was simply a reminder that he had overstepped his lease on the world.

The men walked on ground firmly frozen, staring at the nape of the Permanent in front of them. If they breathed in too deeply, the air that was fresh with clean coolness stung in the bottom of their lungs. The few things a man ceaselessly needed to stay alive: breath, food, sleep, were almost all completely estranged from them, and with winter came a distaste to draw the air that was the only thing in enough quantity for which they did not suffer want. Mirko led his group, as he did when he was on duty during the day. He was just as ignorant of their activity's purpose as they were. He fancied himself among them, not in charge of them; a morbid fancy, as bereft of guilt as it was distant to reality. Mirko shook his head at himself; the beating rhythm of footsteps behind him echoed of bare feet or disintegrating shoes. His were booted warmly. There was nothing to equate. From their stoic mouths came long slow plumes of white breath, breathed out with automatic evenness to prove they were alive. It reminded Mirko of the steam from the paper press in Gregor's cigarette factory.

During his brief encounters with the Commander, Mirko thought he was found out. The razor-sharp pendulum that was his trespass against the forces and very bolts of the camp lowered a centimeter with each gone week. He felt it brushing the top of his uniform shirt just above his stomach, a faint tick as the sharp edge rhythmically came in contact with a button. The Commander was so apt in his ambiguity that each of his gestures, each of his enigmatic commentaries proved that he knew of Mirko's secret evening gifts, and was toying with him, pulling the legs from a trapped spider, before he would crush it under heel.

"What I need from you Erinnerung, is to do your job until it is over. No fence with no amount of electricity will baptize you from this. Stay away from them."

He loved reciting programmed speeches. The Commander must have been an actor before this, Mirko thought, marching along stride for stride with everyone else. He practices his lines to deliver them with cold precision, like an actor excited on opening night but bored each performance after until the end of the run. The only thing devoid in the Commander's voice was any true concern for the well-being of his soldier, insinuated in suggesting Mirko should stay away from the fences.

What Mirko did was wait. He continued meeting the Kapo because the part inside of him that rejected what he was participating in outweighed the part that was afraid for his own life. What he expected from the Commander, the hell of his heel, had not yet come.

"You know of the building?"

"The Frauenkirche? Mirko, I am in part offended that you would ask me about a Christian church and part offended that you think I would not know of one of the most famous icons of our skyline. Yes, Mirko, I know of the Frauenkirche."

"I didn't want to be presumptuous."

"I am certain you didn't want to be. I can see. But yes, of course I know of it."

Mirko thought for a moment. He thought that the Kapo looked better than he had in quite a while. The nights were colder than the days. The obvious absence of sun brought the night its most sheer and frustrating climate, but the two sat shivering together anyway, their backs against the bunker and their eyes at the splattered stars.

"It is the most beautiful thing I've ever seen. My mother, she used to love it. Used to tell my brother that it belonged to us. I never heard her say it to me, of course."

"What happened to her?"

"My mother? How am I to know? They said it was a stroke she had while delivering me. What does it matter? She was gone before I came."

"Did you ever feel guilty?"

"What do you mean?"

"Guilty. I mean that somehow it was your fault what happened to her."

"But it was not."

"I know. But some people, you know. They feel responsible in those situations."

"I see. I did not. I do not. The older I get, the less I find it necessary to place blame for anything on anyone."

"That is very convenient for you."

"Yes. Perhaps it is. But I think back on the Frauenkirche and I don't care."

"What do you mean?"

"It is beautiful, yes?"

"Surely. It is remarkable. I remember being young and looking at it. Of course, I never entered. But I could look at the outside. I'd strain to see the cupola from the ground, though of course I never could. It was beautiful the way it stood there. Remarkable in its construction, in its detail. I was sad my mother never let me enter. Its stone was smooth, I remember that. It curved around elegantly and broke only when shapes rose from it in varied but even places. I remember the windows. The smoothness of the stone."

Mirko nodded.

"But what do you mean, Mirko, when you say that you do not care?"

"It is still there."

"The Frauenkirche?"

"Yes. In Dresden. It is still there."

"Yes, it is. I'm not sure I understand you, Mirko. Perhaps this cold has made your mind freeze. I will find you a burner to put your forehead against and thaw your thoughts." The Kapo laughed to himself.

"No. I mean, it is there now, as it was before today, and as it will be after today. People have walked by that one building for generations. Through everything in history that has happened, it has stood by watching, just as beautiful as the day it was finished. That's what prevents me from feeling too badly about all of this. Not to blame anyone. Not myself, not you, not anyone. This will pass. All of this. It will be a pockmark on our memory, but the Frauenkirche will still stand and it will tell people year after year, decade after decade, century after century until the end of the world, that we were beautiful."

"We?"

"People. Us. It's all there in the stone. The unmovable stone. That despite everything, we are still, at some part, in some place inside of us, beautiful. That is what my mother knew."

"That is what your mother knew."

"It is."

"I think you are right Mirko. That is what that building is. For you, at least, surely. But I understand you now completely."

"Yes."

"Truly." He paused. Then, "Mirko?"

"Yes, Kapo." The Kapo pursed his lips into a smile. It didn't resonate joy as much as it did the comprehension that to Mirko, he would always be *Kapo*, that he would always *have* to be *Kapo*. "I am feeling better. My illness, it wavers."

Mirko smiled at him, "If we survive this, what will we be to each other?"

"The Frauenkirche, Mirko. Each other's."

Chapter 17

Immortality is as frightening as death.

This occurs to me at yet another memorial. Another eternal reminder. South and I picked up where we left off because that's what we should have done. Picked up. The pieces. The garbage. The pace. Whichever. One truth is that after something traumatic, you have no choice but to live on, to find some semblance of everyday life. It is strange, how quickly people return to their routine. But they do. Always. So we do, too. We picked up the next morning and drove clear out to Southern California.

Immortality is as frightening as death. It shocks me what we wish to remember forever; truly, it does.

South mumbles "God," looking at the memorial.

God. If I met Him, what would we discuss? He has no part in this, I know. I do not have the relief of belief. What I have is a lot of plot, my life moving forward in the constancy of one direction. But South mouths the word and just a little sound escapes, tossed at the monument to clink off its granite. The railings lead up to the sculpture like train track rails. Rails for railings. Palm trees rise casually down side streets from every direction around the monument in their strange way, stealing my attention, as do the people who walk by. South stands in the middle of the six pillars, spinning around, reading their inscriptions. I'm fixated on the people wearing shorts here at night, walking their dogs by. So much blond hair, I get chills. Los Angeles is a place people talk about, and I am drawn to its people more so than the pillars that are supposed to represent smokestacks, or the granite ground that is supposed to somehow represent the absorbed blood of the murdered. Supposed to be, everything a metaphor. I am attracted by

all things outside of the monument's eerie circumference:
the fast food restaurant across the street, the passing mo-
torists, bodies maneuvering in the evening. Light shines
through translucent glass by the doors of the closed museum.

This is supposed to symbolize hope.

I can appreciate South in his transient way. He is sudden in his changes. We woke up the afternoon following
our long evening and morning with Bert and Marjorie and
did not mention a word of the experience. I wanted to, but
I could not. It was the coward in me again showing himself.
Or perhaps I was thwarted by the reclamation of my friend
the next morning, who awoke and whistled loudly over the
noise of falling water in the shower. I lay in bed simply
listening to him whistle, the most impossible joyous sound
coming from a man who had just expelled so much. Perhaps that's what it was, the whistle of a free man, burden-
less and enraptured with the extent of his weightlessness.
I do not know. I was lying in the bed tentative after I woke,
noticing that South was in the shower, afraid of what
would be said between us when he exited the shower and
we were face to face once again, tense in the proximity of
an achieved personal closeness. Then there was the sudden whistle. A Spring morning birdsong, flight-sore from
the after-winter travel north, my South, singing in the
shower.

And we drove on, what we've become good at. So late
in my life, and I have found another friend. It amazes me
to think it, even after the time we've spent together. I
never thought I'd have another, after losing the one. I
think if you lose something like that, something that had
been so dear to you, something that helped you survive,
that saved your life; I don't know, I just don't think you ever
believe there will be another to come around. But there
was South, whistling. There we were driving to California,
to Los Angeles, to remember again.

He steps out from among the six pillars and comes over to me, the look on his face suggesting the weariness of travel. Bags under his eyes hold shadows and the muscles of his face are slack. His thick hands remain down at his sides and as he approaches, he rubs his round fingers around the pockets of his jeans, as if he is massaging his own hips.

"It amazes me," he says.

"Everything is a symbol."

"What?"

"The six million casualties, bundled a million to one in the stacks."

South looks around and up at the memorial; in the darkness, they blot out the sky in striated streaks. "I'll be damned. You think that up, yeah?"

I shake my head, gesture to the information plaque.

"Huh," he says, shrugging and walking away. He turns a quarter of the way back to me, eyes me in the periphery, and drums the toes of his right foot in a mute beat. "After, you know, after I found the kid, things happened pretty quickly. It's like my life kept on happening without me. There was a trial, Old Man. And then my wife. And then DC."

I just look right back into his eyes. His shirt has picked up the stains of hasty rest stop meals; I glance at each, colors of condiments and grease spots that speckle the cloth at odd intervals and in odd shapes. I look back into his eyes. He's still there, looking back, letting me filter his words through my screen. It's tough to imagine his ability to be so candid about what so affected him only hours before, but I have to take South as he is, because it is him standing in front of me, enigma or not. I must take him as his portion. Earlier that same day, he was slumped at a bar table, figuring how to tell me his most heavily-weighted secret; and now, here at the memorial, he's as casual as apple pie.

He continues, "Sometimes I think war is just a big fist-fight, yeah? Either way, you try to hurt someone."

I'm cautious and casual. Calm and uncomfortable. I'm defending myself from a lion with only a chair. Mostly, I'm silent.

"I wanted to tell you all along, you know. But I didn't know how to bring it up. How do you tell someone that you've killed someone, especially after everything that happened to *you*? I didn't want you to think, well, I didn't want you to think that I was like them."

"The soldiers."

"Yeah."

"You're not," I say.

"I just maybe sometimes feel like them."

"Trust me, Lombard. I knew the soldiers, perhaps more than anyone. You're not like them at all."

He laughs at himself. I laugh at myself. It sounds like two men laughing at each other, bouncing gladly against the walls of our asylum. "Yeah. Anyways. It's something I have to live with. But I wish I could see my kids."

"Why don't you?"

"Complicated."

"I'm an old man, Lombard. Everything is complicated for me. Waking in the morning, getting from my bed, warming my hands…all complicated. If there's one thing we are, old men, it's patient, because we have to be."

He nods in the recognition that one day he'd comprehend, and says, "My wife. She thinks it's better I spend some time away. That's the whole D.C. thing, yeah? Chief back in Philly had an in with Defensive Driving courses down in Washington and I took it. I had nothing else. I was a fallen hero in Philly, but had the pension." South looks into the light coming up from the museum. "She loves me still, Old Man. That's good. That's the good of it. She thought I needed a change, something to be different before

I could come back. Maybe come back. It must have been hard for her; no matter how many times I heard 'hero,' I didn't believe it. I was different to her, to the kids. So I took it, the Defensive Driving courses, which only run so often and all, so I can spend my time driving all around God's creation with you on this strange road trip."

I am aware of this: South hurts more than he lets on. Deep within him is a guilt that cannot be touched. I see it in his stance, his one-sided slump. I hear it in the questions of his voice. I know the sound because it is also mine. And I know that South will hold onto this guilt, the extreme sensation of it, for the rest of his life. We're inmates, we share a cell, so we know how to commiserate inside of our trespasses. I smile and reach up to pat him on the shoulder. He is tall and my bones creak so the action is histrionic, played out in bad pantomime, but my hand makes it. I pat his shoulder a few times, a masculine but comforting gesture, and when I remove it to allow it to fall back down, it instead—it being its own being—cups against South's cheek. It's only a moment, then gravity keeps its promise and we're both standing there, hands to our sides, facing one another. Two men; two men.

Maybe God did create it all, inasmuch as He created people to go along with everything. To build things then knock them down then build them again. How similar we are, South and I, and he doesn't even know it. It's the easiest thing in the world to be a liar when the truth is so much worse than what we can make up. This is the final thesis of history.

The greyness under my arm never sinks. It floats there, itches every time we approach a memorial like this.

Chapter 18

The ground rumbled with a violence that questioned the sanctity of solidarity in the Earth. The Permanents and soldiers both reached for things to hold on to, to keep themselves upright. It was not an earthquake, but low-flying German planes, heading this way and that, with no particular consistency. To the Kapo, they seemed confused, chaotic, without real direction but instead burning fuel to cover their tracks. They seemed anxious, flying in twos and threes, sometimes in the bundles of obvious formations and sometimes in the littered specs of tired birds, crows in a cockeyed murder. It gave him hope; he smiled to himself, rocking as the Earth seemed to wave like wake trailing a boat. Fluid from the solid. Those planes were flying too low.

Mirko knew it too, but as for what it meant, he could only suppose. The Commander was interestingly vacant more and more as the days went on. He would watch the planes as they flew by, and watch as they returned, and eventually, he would not be present for the morning call. His direct subordinates took up the daily routine. Mirko hadn't seen him for weeks and wondered if he was still at the camp at all. There was a general change in mood, a reversal. The soldiers looked at each other much more often, trying to catch a telling glance from someone's eyes, a suggestion only, that their worst supposition was correct, that it was all almost over, but not over in their best interests. There were many soldiers who were confident in the German cause and filled their roles gladly. Reverberations from the last Great War justified their noble ethnocentrism and made an ugly monster out of the rest of the world. The prospect of Germany falling again at the hands of the same barbarians was perhaps worse than the individual soldier falling in battle. For Mirko, however, it was expected. He felt that Germany would lose the war the first day he was assigned to duty and, in the rain, had to hold his ear to the furniture box-truck while the dog barked its anger at him.

He held on to the top of his rifle like a cane, the butt planted into the soft ground, the anxiety of his fellow soldiers palpable, and almost smiled. "This is the end," he thought. "They move with so much concern. They are scared, the planes. No destination and no home. It will be over soon." He watched the last of them fly by, their fumes so repugnant that he involuntarily scrunched his brow in reaction to them. "Don't think this way," he thought. "Do not become hopeful. Surely they look frightened, but it means nothing. And it is not as if you are not a soldier. Those planes fly for you, in the end. And in the end, when they are out of air in which to move, there may not be any room for you at all." The paradox was a conundrum. He wished for the chaos of the planes but knew it meant the chaos of his life.

So be it.

"Ok, and on! This is not the cinema. March!" yelled a soldier who succeeded in rank in the absence of the Commander. The group began to march to the front of the camp.

The night before, three Permanents from another bunker tried to escape. Mirko was on night duty, though it wasn't a night when provisions were being passed. He was in a watchtower in the Southeast corner of the camp, manning an intense spotlight that he seldom moved, and did so only obligatorily, to propose the suggestion of vigilance. Truly, he did not watch the white spot as it made the color of day in whatever it touched. With a small dull pocket knife, he halved an apple than halved the halves. Then he halved the quarters. Mirko lined the wedges on the wooden railing of the tower, next to the spotlight, and organized them equidistantly and flush from end to end. In succession, he tapped the ends of the wedges closest to him down

the line, making each rock like canoes on a placid lake. He
would wait for them all to settle before he realigned them
and started the fleet again. He had no desire to eat them.
Games like these made the nights bearable, if there was
any fidelity in the term.

The first thing he heard was gunfire. Before the
shouts, before the rushing commotion of movement, he
heard the random popping of gunpowder explosions, of
metal sent spinning down a bore at velocities that separated skin and split bone. His instant reaction was to grab
the rifle and raise the butt to his shoulder, despite the fact
that his instinct was never to kill. He only did it because
that was the only defense there was in war, to raise your
gun. Standing there with the rifle pointed out into the
nothingness of night, he heard a soldier from below call up
to him.

"What are you doing?"

"What?"

"I said, what are you doing? Point the light there."

But Mirko couldn't see the other soldier pointing in the
night. "Where?" he said.

"They're trying to escape, to the other side."

Mirko pointed the spotlight at the other side of the
camp; even though the radius of the beam widened and the
shine diminished the further it went, he still rocked it back
and forth against the fence on the other side of the complex,
a good few hundred yards from his watchtower. He could
see nothing, but no one asked any more of him, so he was
content to continue what he was doing. The firing made
his blood run cold, metal scraped to metal. There were so
many dogs barking that he could scarcely hear anything
but barks and bullets. Eventually, it all sounded the same,
intervals of echoing sounds that never seemed to stop, as
one led into the next and made a blanket sound, a sharp
hum of pursuit and death. He knew the Permanents were
awake, whispering together, huddled, perhaps even trying

to look out of their bunkers at what was happening. The bunker of the Kapo was closest to him, as it was also in the corner of the camp; he imagined the Kapo inside, trying to quiet the men in his bunker, failing to do so. The hum from the distance was loud, but he could imagine the voices down below in startled rapid discourse. The Kapo would be standing amongst them, smaller than most, thinner, with his cowlick spiraling the hair at the top of his head, more noticeable since less attention was spent on hygienic maintenance recently. Though he was only perhaps thirty feet above the Kapo's bunker, Mirko felt at that instant how far away from him he actually was. The realization made him recognize his arrogance. He was a soldier, a warden at a wicked place, and the Kapo was his prisoner. No matter how much, in the past, he had lost this concept—in the delivering of food, in the conversation, in the sharing of friendly cigarettes—the fact remained that they were separate. Polarities. That he was in a watchtower and the Kapo was locked in a bunker. He didn't even know his name; that too, was selfish. He didn't want the burden of knowing a man's name he might have to watch die. Instead, he called him by a word, a title, something that man didn't even want, like the grey numbers under his skin. All things that didn't belong to him but that Mirko ceaselessly gave. And he thought he was the Kapo's friend. Pop pop pop went the other side of camp. Bark bark bark. And Mirko's blood was cold with shame.

He stood there waving the light back and forth until the noises stopped.

It was difficult to concentrate; things were attempting to reform back to order. He saw the movement of soldiers below, at the center of camp, smoking cigarettes and laughing congratulatory praise. So the Permanents who tried to escape dropped their euphemism and became what they were: nothing, Mirko guessed. The jovial nature of the soldiers brought him no comfort; nor did the rest of the evening, the rest of his watch, which went on as most similar evenings did. The adrenaline was drying in his veins, leaving his heart beating quickly and irregularly for no reason and a shallow sickness in his stomach. Of all things, he didn't expect the evening to simply return to normalcy. Of all things, something had to be different that night. But it wasn't. The hum died with its duty done; and despite all of the camp's floodlights at alert, Mirko found it difficult even to remember if any of it had happened at all. So quickly returned the regular.

The next morning, before the planes flew by and shook the Earth so much that Mirko had to steady himself on his rifle, he overheard two soldiers talking. He was supposed to be off-duty the next morning, as he had been on watch overnight, but in light of the escape attempt, all staff were required to be active for the following twenty-four hours.

"From the women's barracks?"

"Yeah. All of them."

"How many?"

"Eight in total. I have to hand it to them, really. You know what they did?"

"No."

"They filed the cement down around the bricks at the bottom of the wall, just the one layer. They were so thin, they flattened themselves out and crawled through."

"Perhaps they're not as stupid as we think."

"What did you think?"

"That they had the intelligence of animals, of course. What else?"

"The men perhaps. The men who sat on their hands when their families were being taken, stupid for sure. But not the women."

"They were taken too, though."

"But they cannot fight. They are women."

"How did they file the cement?"

"Their fingernails."

"You say!"

The other soldier laughed. Mirko did not look at them but side-stepped one meter closer and asked, "How were they found?"

"What?" the first soldier said, noticeably irritated. Mirko had a reputation amongst the other soldiers at camp. He was introverted, considered a misanthrope, despite the irony of the suggestion, and like most people who kept to themselves, was not warmly approached by any of his fellows.

"The women. The eight. How were they found? Found out?"

"Perhaps you helped them, Erinnerung."

"No."

"Where were you last night?" The question was incidental, a snide jab at Mirko, not a true accusation. Mirko knew it, so he didn't feel the need to defend himself, but he stated his alibi anyway.

"The watchtower."

"Well, that's how they were caught. The watchtower. One of them caught her shirt on the fence and shouted, startled, when it got her. All that electricity and no flesh to hold it. The Northeast watch heard, and it was over for them all."

And the planes came, and Mirko leaned on his gun. And the commanding officer in the absence of the Commander told the lines to march on. Only hours before, there was an escape attempt, but it seemed as if nothing had ever happened. The only evidence was in the eight vacancies in the women's line on the other side of camp.

Perhaps it was the planes that made Mirko bold, dizzy flying that signified the end of the war. Or it was the whisperings while soldiers were eating. Attempted desertions.

It could have been the confidence on the faces of the Permanents, who were also aware of the change in atmosphere. The absence of the Commander. The change in regiment: daily work marches were discontinued—temporarily, it was said—in favor of having the Permanents remain in their bunkers for the majority of the day. It may have been too hopeful. But what could have made Mirko bolder was the fact that fewer provisions were being supplied to the Permanents from the soldiers. The food rations for the Permanents were scarce before, but in the recent time of uncertainty, when whispers dominated the forms of speech, the young soldiers didn't focus on their charge, feeding the Permanents not nearly as much. It was enough if they could receive food to feed themselves.

Mirko stood in the Kapo's bunker, by the door, while a routine inspection was taking place. It happened frequently; most of the time it was the Kapos themselves who did the inspections, rummaging through the sparse belongings of the Permanents, exposing paraphernalia to soldiers; but since the planes and the escape attempt, it was the soldiers doing the searches. The bunkers seemed endless, little red houses of brick and brown houses of wood, with lonely brick fireplace steeples protruding from the roofs and only one entrance and exit. They stretched out the entire distance of the visible camp, more bunkers than there were soldiers, so the inspection process never seemed to stop. It was out of one bunker and into the next, and so on. Because there was no more marching, no more work detail, the soldiers were kept busy with such inspections. They often found nothing, but searched again and again, perhaps looking for reasons to continue searching.

On occasion, Mirko would be on a round that would include the searching of the Kapo's bunker. Protocol had it that one soldier would guard the front door while the other two made rounds through the line of Permanents, who were to stand at the end of their bunks and submit to any orders from the inspectors.

As Mirko stood at the door with his rifle leaned against his shoulder and two other soldiers checking the bunks of the Permanents, he felt the eyes of the men on him. They knew him and trusted him. They ate his rotten food once a week, in the middle of the night. Not much, but a surge of energy, the wonderful way food tastes to the starving. They all eyed him without debonairness, a recognition of thankfulness. But also, of expectation. Mirko could see the Kapo at the other side of the bunker. Unlike the other Permanents, the Kapo kept his eyes forward, sure to not look over at Mirko. The sidelong glances of the other men flickered at him, flashbulbs snapping at spontaneous random intervals.

The Permanent closest to him, to his right, at the foot of the first bunk, whispered as quietly as he could, "We are hungry." His voice was raspy, the wind whistling through his whisper. It whined a pitch higher than he would have liked, carrying the volume. Mirko kept his head forward but shifted his eyes to the man and shook his head back and forth minimally but quickly.

"We are hungry," the man said again, "when will we eat again?" His name was Leonard. He was hunched over, the ridge of his back tenting the back of his shirt as if his spine had turned in on itself. It was almost grotesque, a parody of human body. His shoulders shoved up to his chin and the full extent of his torso raised as it bent forward. From the profile, Leonard looked like a question mark. The human form, confused. Mirko remembered when the man had first come to the camp. He seemed so much younger then, so much straighter. Mirko shook his head again.

"Will you bring us food tonight? We cannot stand without anything." Mirko saw then that the Kapo had noticed the conversation and was looking down the line of bunks at Leonard, willing him quiet with his eyes. But Leonard did not see the warning in the Kapo, nor did he desist when Mirko did not respond. He raised his hands and clasped them together into a pitched roof of prayer, "Please," he said. "Tonight, yes. Bring us something." His voice was now on the brink of audible. Permanents around him began looking down at the line as well, not in reaction but in waiting. The soldiers making the inspection had come around the end of the bunker and were now making their way along the wall to Mirko's right, where at the end, the pleading Permanent still had his hands clasped together. He was sure to be heard. The man was desperate and could not be calmed by ignoring him.

"Be quiet," Mirko mouthed at Leonard.

"Say you will. You are good for us. You are not like them. Please, say you will. Bring us something."

"I will," Mirko said, but the man heard no conviction in it.

"Say you will," Leonard said again. "Please." And Mirko knew that he had to be sincere in order to say it sincerely. He wasn't even on the night shift that evening, and food for the soldiers was becoming scarce as well. It wasn't as easy to dig up leftover and rotting food to supply to the Kapo's bunker because there simply wasn't any around. But he knew he had to be sincere in saying that he would to quiet the man.

The inspecting soldiers were only a few bunks down, halfheartedly moving around the spent blankets of the Permanents with the ends of their rifles. Mirko knew he had to get Leonard to be quiet in seconds. Leonard was shivering, his hands palmed in front of him, looking straight at Mirko. He almost made to step forward toward Mirko when Mirko looked over at him and said, "I will." This time, it was with conviction. Mirko would have to come that evening. He could not have said it so convincingly without it being true.

Mirko would come that evening.

Leonard, sated, put his hands to his side, but kept shaking when the soldiers rifled through his things.

"It was close, yes," the Kapo said, "I was worried for a moment. But we are too scared, you and I. It is as if we are committing a crime, the way we cower."

"But we are," Mirko said.

"And against whom?"

"This place."

"Then I am guilty and happy to be."

Through the cover of night, the Kapo couldn't see Mirko's reaction, which trembled with the distaste of the situation. It was far too close, Leonard approaching him directly like that, with other soldiers only a few yards away. Mirko sensed the end of the war and had developed the misfortunate hope that he would now somehow survive. He paced slowly behind the bunker, exhausted from yet another long shift outside of the extra-laborious hours as a soldier in the terminal camp.

"Settle down, Mirko. What is concerning you?"

"That man. That stupid man."

"It is over."

"Yes, but it was too close."

"So much happens in proximity, truly. You know this. What is it really, Mirko? What makes you this way?"

Mirko thought to himself, too distracted to have heard the Kapo's question. The tension in the camp winded through him, tightly coiled, the potential energy stored menacingly in his stomach. He could feel the boot-steps of lines advancing his way. Soon was to be a great change. When it came down to it, Mirko was afraid for his life; the certainness of his end supplanted his hope of resilience. Doom approached with tanks.

"What do you miss most of Dresden?" he asked the Kapo.

"Dresden?"

"Yes. Your home. What do you miss about it while you are here?"

"My home? I do not think of it."

"Why?"

"I cannot."

"You mean it is too painful?"

"No, I mean I cannot think of it. All I can see when I close my eyes is this place. It is the only thing that exists."

"This is not so for me. Dresden exists."

"I am sure it does. But I cannot think of it."

Mirko lit a new cigarette and inhaled too deeply from the first drag, the sulfur from the match sinking into his lungs with the tobacco smoke and burning him deep in his chest. He pulled open the end of his jacket and buried his face inside, trying to mute the inevitable cough that came with explosions of fire in his esophagus. He coughed twice only, the smoke filling his self-made enclave and stinging his eyes. He resurfaced from the inside to hear a shuffling from an adjacent bunker. He and the Kapo both looked in the direction of the bunker, remaining silent and still, to hear if there was to be a second sound. The only thing moving was the smoke from the ends of their cigarettes, which rose with delicate fluidity into the evening, where it became invisible. They remained like this for a few minutes, hearing nothing.

"Did you?" Mirko asked, cutting his own obvious question short.

"Yes."

No further sound issued into the evening.

"My family," said the Kapo.

"What?"

"My family. That is what I miss. The family that lived in Dresden."

"You will see them. I think it will be soon."

The Kapo laughed but there was nothing jovial about it, "You're faith is admirable Mirko, but you are perhaps too quick to presume them alive."

"Would they be too quick to presume you dead? If you are here, then it is possible that they too are alive, missing you and being as cynical about your fate."

The Kapo smiled but it was too dark for Mirko to see the reaction that his comment provoked. "Not all of them will survive."

"But some."

"Maybe. But do you propose to win over my pessimism with the suggestion that only some of my family will perish in this?"

"What else would you have me do?"

"Nothing, Mirko. I would have you do nothing more."

"Kapo."

"I know no such name. We are more than our insignias," the Kapo said, gesturing to the symbol on Mirko's sleeve.

"We are."

"Perhaps we are more than anything that we are."

"What do you mean?"

"I don't know, I just talk." The Kapo thought he heard another sound coming from the adjacent bunker but presumed it to again be his imagination. "What of your family, Mirko?"

"There isn't much."

"Quantity does not depreciate value."

"No. There is Adette."

"Your sister."

"Yes. She remains in Dresden. I have no doubt that it is hard for her, being alone with no support."

"But you do support her."

"I haven't written."

"I don't mean with words. In your thoughts."

"That is not adequate support."

"Perhaps not. But I am sure she values it nonetheless."

"Could we not speak of Adette?"

"Of course."

"She used to teach me the Bible, you know."

"So you *do* wish to talk of her."

"No. Forget it."

"Okay. I will tell you though, Mirko."

"Is it about Adette? Because I don't want to hear it."

"No. It is about Germany."

"Oh, what of Germany? What of this terrible country?"

"A country is not as terrible as its government. I am a German too, remember. Do not offend my patriotism."

"You joke now."

"A little. But I was as proud a German as the administration itself. I too suffered under the *Peace Treaty*. I too awaited the retribution that was surely to result from its development. I just never presumed. . ."

"That it would be in this form?"

"Against our own. Against Germans themselves. It makes me sad. Mirko, do you think the world will ever know the good that was Germany before all of this?"

"No."

"It is lost?"

"It has to be. It is killed."

"You are good, Mirko, but I think you are wrong."

"I am worried about your man," Mirko said. He had been since the encounter earlier that day. Mirko fashioned a plan to steal the food; he fashioned a plan to be behind the bunker at night despite the fact that he had no reason to be there that evening, despite the fact that the watchtower would be manned by someone else. He had relieved that soldier, said he couldn't sleep. Said he would take his shift. He was not met with antagonism. He had completed all of these steps to be able to deliver the food and complete his sincere promise to the arch-spined man, but he still maintained the worry that Leonard would not wait much longer, that hunger would inspire his insubordination to the point where Mirko would have to act. That was his fear, that he would be forced to reprimand the man in order to keep his secret safe, and that there was no reprimand he could administer short of killing him. If not, Leonard would surely let the secret be known. This potential frightened Mirko so totally that he was anxious throughout the day, and talking with the Kapo just then outside of the bunker, he wanted nothing more than to give him the food he found and be done with it.

"He waits. He has taken this most recent famine harder than most."

"I have only this," Mirko said, picking up the familiar canvas bag and withdrawing from it a half of a loaf of bread and assorted vegetables in various stages of decay.

"It is good," the Kapo said, taking it.

From the adjacent bunker came a low whine that rose with quick crescendo into a human yell that staggered in segregated words to form a sentence just comprehensible. "There. There. Is. Food. Please!" The voice staggered high in its desperation. It was a howl, a wolf snarl full of envy and the ends of humanity.

Mirko and the Kapo looked at the bunker but could see almost nothing in the dark. They looked at each other as well, but could not see each other's expressions. Even so, they both knew, without seeing. Without seeing, they had been seen.

From the other bunker, a Permanent had his eye at a small gap between wood planks that separated just enough to allow him to look out. In the winter, it was this small separation in the wood that chilled him so deeply that he'd press the pad of his foot onto the crack to prevent the cold from coming in. Awakened by the cough from outside, the Permanent turned around on his wooden bunk and pressed his eye to the crack. What usually afforded him a view of the corner of camp, two barbed wires of an electric fence meeting at a concrete post, then provided him with the view of a German soldier providing a Kapo with food. His eyes were adjusted to the dark as they had become accustomed inside of his eyelids, and although all he could see were silhouettes, the tall boxy figure of a soldier's uniform and the weakly disheveled outline of a Permanent were evident to place the people.

The man had yelled, uncontrollably, insanely. In the otherwise silence, the words traveled with velocity, the words preceding a constant and erupting yell from the man that woke up a fury of murmuring: Permanent after Permanent. Bunker after bunker.

Soldier after soldier.

Mirko and the Kapo stood there with complete knowledge of the circumstance. The Permanent's voice from the other bunker and the commotion it invoked was as loud as any alarm in the camp. They had been careful, but there was only so much care one could take in a place of such carelessness.

"Mirko."

"Kapo, I..." But he could say nothing more. The Kapo found him in the dark and embraced him, simply and kindly. His hands were fists against Mirko's shoulder blades, the embrace a fragile gesture at the end.

CHAPTER 19

It got out of control before I could control it.

I think it is a part of us, us people, to hope beyond reason for absolution. People expect, up to the last, that their nightmares will be relinquished with the crowing cock. Standing there in the evening of the camp, in the midst of mist, with the echoed words of the Permanent who saw our trespass swallowed in the rising loudness of action coming to meet us, I thought, somehow, that everything would be all right. It was perhaps a moment of weakness that denied the empirical rationality that our fortune had emptied to the bottom of its barrel; we were caught, stuck, birds in cages, bolts in a machine that cranked and clicked until its rust sunk into the lungs of the Earth, and mixed with the ashes. But for a moment, standing there with my friend, I felt hope. The painful, thievish, inaccurate, magical, desperate, uncanny, megalomaniacal, abstract, unconditional, dramatic, triumphant, consistent, beautiful repose of hope.

Here, now, South has lost himself, busy looking for my number in the pillars. Again, pillars. Again, symbols of smokestacks. I wonder at the wonder that is ingenuity when it comes to the preservation of artifacts of memory. There is so much sameness in honor. I have heard it said numerous times that those who forget history are doomed to repeat it. I suppose I do not have much of an objection to the cliché, but the bliss I would feel for a moment of forgetfulness would be a value almost expensive enough to chance the spiraling years to meet on end and repeat themselves over and over. Memorials litter the landscape, but new wars roll flat old terrain and make way for more symbols of memory. So long as our foresight is shielded by squinting, it seems we will be doomed with repetition despite how crystal-clear the hindsight.

At first, I wouldn't let South see, but he pleaded almost down to his knees. "It's important," he said.

"Why?"

"To see."

In a way, it seems he is fact-checking. Invoicing. Making sure the numbers match. I eventually relented and lifted my sleeve. South mouthed the words that matched the digits then marched to the pillars. I do not enter the corridor of them after South, but look after him, afraid. I am afraid he won't find my number on any of the stacks and will then conclude that I am not me. Of course, we will just come to the conclusion that Boston arbitrarily put numbers on the stacks to symbolize the people, or South's eyes will get dizzily distorted with the exhaustion of reading, or he will be hungry for a burger and beer, or something. Still, I am apprehensive with his checking up on me.

But perhaps I do deserve to be punished. My life is wrong, of all things. I feel it in my body's persistence to wake up every morning. Every day, I am met with the disappointment that I have survived another night. Because I know *his* name. But no, I've survived nothing. I am a burning flame, not alive but hot and singeing anything that approaches, blackening a wick and melting wax. I am a beautiful thing capable of much destruction. That, then, is the symbol for us all. A flame. Baltimore got it right, all the way back there at the beginning. A flame that is us. Us of a flame. Majesty in its design, treachery in its power.

We are fire.

The stacks are made of translucent blue glass, of the same height, and are equidistant. The numbers are etched into the glass. South can't possibly read them all. But he stands there anyway, his right hand clasping the wrist of the left behind his back, as if he's in an art museum pretentiously assuming to comprehend the artist's intent. His interest is childlike and, as if I am his parent, I can't imagine tearing him away from his task. Read away, Lombard.

The majority of numbers are much higher than he can see, but he likes his chances. He looks over at me as if to recall the numbers themselves. Perhaps he's found them, or has come close. Ultimately, he goes back to the pillar, convinced that I'm there somewhere, etched into the blue.

The drive back to the East Coast did not seem as long as the drive out. In part, this was due to the fact that we didn't stop nearly at all. We stopped to eat or rest, and South took to photographing the signs of new states that we passed into.

"I wish I would have thought of this before now," he had said, lumbering into a thick uncropped shrubbery to shoulder up next to *Welcome to Wyoming* with the subtitle *Equal Rights* at the bottom of the sign. "Damn shame to see so many states and not have the proof to say you were there, yeah?"

I found it difficult to say I had *been* to a place that I only drove through.

Iowa was tricky. Its welcome sign hung above the interstate on a metal rigging that had to be at least twenty-five feet from the ground. South pulled over as we approached it.

"South. No," I said.

"When's the next time we'll be in Iowa, yeah?" he replied.

We got out of the car on the shoulder and South strode right up to the metal rigging that touched down just outside of the blacktop on the loose, light brown dirt. He began inspecting the structure and I knew that he was contemplating the best form of ascent. South is a fit young man, by all means, but I imagined him falling over and over, from that height, all to get a picture. And there I would be, old and slow, having no idea how to drive the car in which I had just spent so many hours.

It took me a while to snap the correct picture, as the sun was behind him and whitewashing every digital exposure, but I eventually got it. South in sunglasses and the biggest, worst smile on his face. Iowa. *Our Liberties We Prize and Our Rights We Will Maintain.*

In almost every sense, it was a comfortable journey back. Of course, I had never approached the East from that direction, and I imagined the ocean rushing toward me while Lombard sped toward it. For South, there was the expedited measure of getting home, or, to some semblance of home. He was an East Coast guy, as he told me quite frequently. Yeah? He was on his way home, barreling over the country while its mysterious ways changed back to normal. It amazed me how much it had stayed the same since we left.

I asked him if we could go to Philadelphia on the way home. He said *I don't know.* I understood him completely; I didn't want to see Dresden either, though I'm sure my reasons are different.

I do Boston and all the other cities an injustice by being so critical of the symbolism and the goal of organizations that raise these monuments because I know the intent is good. It is beautiful, really, the clear day and the light shining through the blue glass. The harbor water salty to smell. Strange accents that remotely sound like South's. Husbands and wives arm in arm while their children slalom in chase of one another through the stacks, here to sightsee just off the Freedom Trail. A sight to see.

"I couldn't find it," South says to me, stepping carefully over the grates of the memorial, which make him "uncomfortable" to walk on. This is something I've learned of South. One of the many things I've learned about him. Idiosyncrasies that when learned, beget intimacy. South sleeps on his stomach and likes his feet hooked off the end of the bed. South is left-handed but writes right. South performs the same outdated stretches every morning, limbering only select muscles, as if he were an extra in a workout video from the 1980s. South steals glances at children with their fathers. And so on. It would seem like so little to a casual observer to recognize how much I've learned of South having spent so much time with him, but truly, my discovery of him is an epiphany for me, something I haven't felt in a long time.

"No?"

"Your number, I couldn't find it."

"I see."

"It's probably one of those little bastards up there, yeah?" South says, pointing to numbers at the high end of the nearest stack.

"Maybe."

"It is. Or else they're just fake numbers. But would they do that, do you think?"

"They could have."

"Oh well. I wanted to find them. To see. But it's not like they recorded your numbers off the boat or anything right?"

South is not an ignorant man. There was no boat, despite his perhaps romantic American notion that I and thousands of other refugees gazed longingly on a barge at South Manhattan from the harbor outside of Ellis Island. Nor do I remember anyone checking for my number. I barely remember anything really. Just that, after years of things moving very slowly, suddenly, things were moving very quickly. And one day, I was in D.C. And one day, South held the door open for me at our building. And one day, I was in a car driving through the country that made a history out of my home.

"Lombard?"

"Old Man?"

"I always think about my friend."

Lombard pauses to let a family pass by. "From the camp?"

"Yes."

"Do you remember his number?" He gestures over to the stacks, "We can look. . ."

"No. It is not there."

"You're right, they probably just put random numbers up there anyway." South is careful with me. "Tell me about him."

"I haven't spoken a word about him in all of these years. I don't know if I can now."

"Try."

I do it only because of how much South reminds me of him. Not the personality, or the physique, or anything really. But the way he makes me feel in my time of struggle. Because, if I admit it to myself, I am struggling now, as I have been ever since my symbolic boat met the harbor. And like my friend, South brings me peace when there is none.

"He was young."

"And you?"

"I was young, too. Maybe even the same age."

"But he died."

"Yes, Lombard." He is not being insensitive. South's brand of reality is forceful; he is a psychotherapist's nightmare. "He died."

"So, was he German too?"

"Yes. He was actually from where I am from."

"Germany?"

"Dresden."

"Dresden?"

"A small city in the East."

"I haven't heard of it."

"I don't doubt it."

"So you knew him, before. . .it all?"

"No."

"Really? That's weird."

"Dresden isn't a small European village, Lombard. It's a city. Big as D.C."

"Oh."

"Can we sit down?"

"Sure, Old Man. You hungry? We can go to one of those pubs?" He points over to the colorful row of bars that line the street and I nod. We make our way over, enter one, and find a small wooden elevated table by the door, flanked on both sides by wooden bar stools with green linoleum plush seat cushions. We sit. I have the feeling that we are at the end of our journey.

The bartender comes out from behind the bar and asks us if we'll have menus. South says yes and orders two beers.

"I always had a question about one thing, yeah?" South says. He's opening up now that I'm opening up. Two flowers, first spring. I do not think he's had an ulterior motive, but I've known he's had questions all along. I suppose anyone would. You meet someone who has lived through the most famous atrocity in human history and you have a few questions. All your acquaintances become detectives.

"Ok, Lombard, ask me."

"No. I mean, it's a messed up question. I don't want to be rude and all, about it."

"It's okay."

"You sure?"

I nod.

"So they really used showers like they talk about? With gas?"

"I never had the personal experience, but I knew of them. They were there."

"So your friend?"

"Not that way."

"Oh."

"Lombard, it's because of him that I am alive today. He kept me alive enough to get through it. His being there. I am here for it. And I am also responsible for his death."

South shakes his head and bunches up his mouth to one side as if he disapproves and is subsequently disappointed in my failure to be accurate. "You didn't kill him."

Just then the bartender comes over with our drinks and there is the awkward hanging of those last words resounding over the table while he sets down the glasses and we pause. When the bartender walks back behind the bar, I respond, "Lombard."

"Well, you didn't. It was those bastards."

I can smell the cigarette smoke of his breath out there in the wonderful night of the camp, the fumes rising out of his mouth without him blowing them, then the smile as he shuts his mouth and forces them from his nostrils like a bull. Such an anachronistic smile, something that didn't belong in that place, but was there. In defiance of it. Our proximity, against the walls of a bunker. We had thought that there was a future for us as old men remembering. But here I am, an old man, only remembering through memorials erected by subsequent generations, who substitute my hopeful gone remembrances with symbols. He was a real person. But I am here now, and he exists only in the memory of the man who caused his transience.

South looks up to me and says, "I'm going to get a burger. Big surprise, yeah?"

"Yeah, Lombard."

"Only damn thing on the menu that looks good anymore."

CHAPTER 20

Mirko tried to not think of his father, but he often did. Dead before Mirko was born, his father was seldom mentioned in the small apartment in Altstadt, and became a phantom for the family, something that haunted perhaps more because it was ignored.

In the camp, there were long stretches of lonely time when Mirko ignored the announcements of the loudspeakers and thought of his father. He couldn't have been that much older than me, Mirko would think. Somewhere in Russia, or France, or somewhere; somewhere anywhere but home. Somewhere face down, or face up, eyes at the sky for the final moment. Or apart, in pieces. Modern warfare. Mirko didn't like to think of this; in his fabricated memories, his father was always whole, perhaps a simple small hole in his body, enough to let everything out. Perhaps he was a pilot, or a tank driver. No, Mirko's father would have been a soldier on foot, like Mirko himself was. He was young and fearful and didn't want to be where he was. He had two small children at home and another coming.

Mirko didn't expect Gregor to tell him anything, as Gregor was also too young to have any information himself. Children are never told the truth, as they are deemed too fragile, too vulnerable for truth. Of course, all children know better; children are limber, more accepting. It's when they live under illusions for so long that their spirits are broken with revelation. So much trouble could be saved if they didn't have to find out about the horrors of the world surprisingly, shocked with adolescence, Mirko thought. Both parents, permanent tragedies: a war of the world and a war of the body. In the end, it was all war. Things fighting things, things tumbling into crumbling.

Gregor was the closest thing Mirko ever had to a father, and he was gone, too.

Mirko, however, was not. He sat in the office of the Commander with the door shut behind him and two sentries guarding outside. The Commander sat quietly across from him. Mirko was not bound, nor was he physically harassed or detained. The Kapo had tried to rush back into his bunker, but the other guards, anxious for another escape attempt, almost hoping for it, so that they could again vent their anxiety, were there too quickly. He was caught entering his bunker. Mirko was asked calmly, a few hours later, to join the Commander in his office.

He had not seen the man up close in quite a while. The Commander, Mirko now supposed, spent the majority of his time in the office, which smelled of hard liquor. The Commander refilled a long thin tumbler from the well of the glass to the brim, spilling the contents over every time, and drank back to back. War spirits were cheap spirits, and they burned his throat perfectly, exactly what he wanted. The razing burn of pleasure. While Mirko watched, the Commander finished off the remainder of the whiskey in the glass and promptly refilled it. His hair had the ignored look of drunks who could care less about what their hair looked like. He seemed completely composed, sitting across the desk, looking directly at Mirko and moving otherwise only to sip from the glass.

The two sat there awkwardly. Mirko exchanged glances with the Commander and the top of his desk, not knowing what would happen but knowing well enough that something would. I have lasted a long time, Mirko thought. Doing this. And I don't feel bad to die for it now. That could be the only course; his life would be stolen. Fitting for the regime that built this machine. But strangely, having recognized his own peril, and having accepted it for a final truth, Mirko did not feel fear. Of course, his body reacted *ad nauseam* with nausea, his stomach weakly grumbling and his extremities subtly shaking, but his mind was controlled and accepting. Bold to face the worst the Commander could do to him.

It would be quick. It always was. This machine did not have time to waste on pomp.

The Commander sat there with the tumbler loosely surrounded by his left hand while the right cupped the side of his face, his fingertips just entering the field of his disturbed hair. He was leaning down on it, with his elbow on the table. Mirko looked into his eyes. They were present, disappointed. Mirko wondered if that was how a father looked at a son with whom he was disappointed. He thought not; through the disappointment, there would be love there, too.

Still, the Commander didn't say anything. Mirko could hear the shuffling of the guards outside. They shuffled like all the guards shuffled. No one could stand still anymore, even those who truly believed in what they were doing. Everyone knew what was coming—dogs sensing earthquakes.

In one force, the Commander raised his left hand and tipped back the glass against his bottom lip, letting the brown liquid rush freely into his throat. He swallowed in one tremendous gulp and placed the glass gently back on the desktop. For a moment, the smile that Mirko had seen mischievously placed on the Commander's face so often during his time at the camp, flickered in the muscles of his mouth, then died with the futility of a wick trying to relight itself. Minus the stale whiskey smell, it was like the first time Mirko sat in the office. Resonant echoes of what Gregor made him promise, to make Germany great, bounced in failed shame inside his head, volleyed ear to ear.

As the Commander reached for the pistol on his waistband, Mirko thought that finally, he had done what Gregor had really wanted. The Kapo was a German, a member of the German people, who are good. Good people. Good people with some evil inside of them. Just like every other person on the planet. For the rest of his life, which seemed to be only seconds, Mirko would feel a moment of relief in recognizing this fact. There are people. There is good in them. There is evil in them. There is circumstance. And there is choice.

Mirko had chosen; and sitting there, with the Commander and his pistol drawn, the choice calmed his stomach, stilled his trembling fingers.

A strange man, Mirko thought, to do this here in his office. But he must be drunk, and it is near the end. For me *and* for him, so it doesn't matter. Whatever there is of me on the walls will either stay until the end, or he will have it wiped away. I can't imagine he is squeamish anymore, all things considered. Still, it is strange. Mirko remembered what Gregor had said when he heard his own earthquake coming: what people, people are.

The Commander pulled back the hammer on his pistol and placed the butt of the gun onto the table, the snout of the beast aimed up at Mirko's chest. Mirko looked at the Commander, directly in his eyes, and breathed normally. He didn't think. He didn't relive his life, his childhood running around the Frauenkirche in beloved Dresden, the late lessons with Adette, the clandestine moments with the Kapo. He didn't think at all. He just waited patiently for the snout's report, and whatever was on the other end of it.

"Miracle," the Commander said. "The English word of an English language that is so soft. Your nickname is as soft as the people who invented its language. Mirko the Miracle. The true name not even German and the false one, English." The pistol was still pointed at Mirko's heart, the hammer still pulled and locked down, back from the bullet's pin, but filled with animosity. "To think I thought I could reform you."

Mirko breathed evenly.

The Commander closed his eyes halfway.

He lifted the gun from the desk and pointed it, with his arm outstretched, at Mirko's face. The Commander then

twisted his own head forcibly to the right, as if to shield it
from the oncoming mess. He looked back at Mirko, smiled
the usual way, and turned the pistol on himself, pointing
the snout at his own temple. The absurdity of it confused
Mirko but he did not show his hand. Mirko did not think
the Commander was going to shoot himself but he didn't
put it beyond him. Either way, Mirko would not play by
the Commander's rules. He would not react.

The Commander laughed twice forcefully and removed
the pistol from his temple. He lowered the hammer with
his thumb slowly so that it was in its benign position and
removed the clip from the pistol's handle. From the clip the
Commander withdrew one of the small bullets, and placed
it, standing upright, on the desk between them. He replaced the clip into the pistol and put it away in the holster
at his waist.

Between them, Mirko thought the bullet looked very
small. A tiny thing that was the end of so many things. It
sat there between them, its destructive end pointing at the
ceiling. The Commander sat back on his chair, reached to
the floor next to him and, retrieving the bottle, poured himself another full glass into the tumbler. He sipped.

They sat in chairs equidistant from the bullet in the
center of the desk. It stood between them, almost taller
than both of them, a condensed capsule of power. Neither,
however, looked at it but from periphery. Its presence, and
the gleam from the lamp in the corner of the desk that reflected off of the bullet, was enough to announce it was
there. That, and its potential.

The Commander, returning Mirko's look directly, sat
forward and said, "This bullet will pass through one human
head," he said. "You will choose, Miracle."

Chapter 21

"I don't know what to tell ya," South says.

I shrug, my eyebrows raised curious.

"I kinda feel that I have to say sorry, yeah?"

"Sorry?"

"Well. I mean. It's not really that dynamic."

"No."

I'm glad for it, for the Holocaust Memorial here in Philadelphia. At least it's distracting South from what we came here for.

"It sort of looks like shit, yeah?"

I keep my shoulders raised shrugging.

"I mean like real shit," South continues. "Like, it looks like a piece of shit."

We didn't leave Boston immediately. South and I had too many beers and I began thinking, after only my second time being intoxicated, that I had to start slowing down. Settling down. I haven't shaved since we left, on account that I had forgotten a razor, and I began to fear people would think I was a vagrant. South suggested we buy a new razor at one of the rest stops but I rejected the idea. The concept of buying something I already had, despite its distance from me, was something I couldn't justify. In all of my life, this is the first time I am traveling for leisure, if there is any merit in considering it such. When you are an inexperienced traveler, such as myself, it's easy to forget what to bring. It's easy to forget what to remember. My razor is rusting away on the small plastic shelf behind my hinge-swung bathroom mirror, and I have developed a white restless beard that rebels from the civility of my otherwise simple face.

I wasn't really that intoxicated. I learned my lesson from New Mexico. Instead, I let him beat me two or three to one; he drank the beers like water, like he was thirsty. People need to round out sharp edges; some people use memorials, others use beer. At the end of our stay at the small bar across from Boston's memorial, South realized that he was too drunk to carry on. He wasn't the sloppy contrite fool from the last time, but he knew his own ability. That's one thing I'll say about South, he's certainly responsible enough. Perhaps it's his old detective days. Maybe there's still a part of him somewhere deep that must obey the law at all costs. Or, at some costs.

I don't feel as old as I did before I met South. I know my body cannot perform the majority of what I ask of it and I am aware of the energy leaving it. I have been close to death before; there have been moments of my life when I could almost assume that my time was through, and there was a feeling in it. It was strange and almost indescribable. I was sure that I was going to die and upon me seemed to drop a clear cool white sheet that touched my body in every place simultaneously. It was a comfort, a cool warming support, and at first, I didn't realize what I was feeling. But there it was, death's prelude, the calmest shut-eyed acknowledgment that my clock's rotations were spiraling down. I was sure I was going to die, and the all-comforting white sheet was cool against all of my skin. But, of course, I didn't die. I didn't survive, but I lived. I don't feel anything of the white sheet now. I am not as wasted as when South met me; his companionship has brought me that much, but I am still a weakening old man. The same spirit children feel entering them in their daily growth, I feel leaving me in my daily decline; but I know I am not close enough to death because I will know this when the cool white sheet again warms me everywhere.

I do not derive any particular pride in knowing this. Sometimes I think to die would be more appropriate. I am not a faithful man, but most faiths believe there will be some sort of judgment after death, and that is what I'm looking forward to.

What South and I did after leaving the bar and his determining that he couldn't drive, was walk around Boston for what seemed like hours. I didn't mind walking and he didn't mind walking slowly, so we made a fine pair. We left the downtown area and ended up in a neighborhood called Southie, which South said reminded him a lot of home.

"Philadelphia?" I asked.

"Philly," he responded.

"Why?"

"It has that old feel, yeah? Like that old neighborhood feel. You don't get that in D.C., Old Man, and I miss that, living down there and all. Do you feel it?" South took a deep breath and brushed his fingertips against the nearest red brick wall, the same fingertips attached to the man who just circled the perimeter of his great country. "You don't get that feeling everywhere. It feels like it knows. That's the only way I can describe it, that it feels like it knows. It's so old, it just has to know everything. This wall, these streets. Man, Old Man, they've got to know it all." South then looked at me with a snarky grin, "Old like you pal, and you know everything, too."

"Not really, Lombard."

"You say. But I hear you talking. You have more words of English in that head of yours than most people in America."

"That's okay, because English isn't American."

"What?" South asked, genuinely confused.

"Nothing."

"Okay. Anyway. This place knows. You can feel it if you let it. But that's what you have to do Old Man, you have to let it."

"I understand."

"You do, yeah? Or are you just saying that to shut me up?"

"No, I do. I came from a place like that. Like this. Like Philad—Philly."

"Dresden. Just like your friend."

"Right, just like my friend. We were both from a place like this. A place that had old bricks too."

"You ever want to go back? To see it? Dresden and all?" South spoke to me but looked all around himself at the neighborhood that was almost his namesake. A brief wind ruffled the opened flap of his unzipped jacket and although it was only momentary, he placed both hands gently on each flap to settle them, his most unconscious movements always presenting the best of him.

"I can't."

"Why?"

"It's gone."

We got plenty lost in Southie. The streets were confusing, and any hope of backtracking seemed impossible, so we ambled forward. My knees began hurting and I when I told South as much, he suggested that he was then fine to drive. The dilemma was that we were then quite far from our car and had no idea how to get back. It was getting late in Boston, already dark, and there were fewer and fewer people out. When we asked someone how to get back downtown, the man responded, "T." South and I just looked at him. He turned and pointed down the street a bit, said "T" again, and we saw a large sign jutting from a building that in fact had the letter "T" illuminated. We approached; it was a subway stop. D.C. has a metro system, though I'd never ridden in, and South didn't trust it. He said that he didn't like traveling where he couldn't see where he was going, though he's generally not paranoid. At the time, it didn't seem like we had much of a choice, so we went underground and made use of the map as best as we could, and took a train back downtown.

Once there, we were just as confused as we were in Southie, but there seemed to be more people around, so it took us only about a half hour to locate our car parked on a side street that I felt I'd never seen before. The labyrinth of downtown Boston, seemingly always shifting. Our chest muscles were tense until we reached the highway.

"Is Philly that confusing?" I had asked South.

"No way, Old Man. Philly's a grid, yeah? A big bunch of squares. Couldn't get lost if you tried."

Again with bronze contortions.

A terrible weight applies to a supine man, who struggles against striations of wood, whereupon bald ghosts of children reach confusedly out. It is in the midst of a small park, uninviting to pedestrians and flanked by the rising mirrored sides of enormous buildings that make me feel trapped in their enclosure. Random swords strike with the strident din of cast metal into the sky and what I notice are the hands reaching out from the melee. They grope, at arm's length, at nothing, at me.

South looks over at me and says, "Okay." And I know it means that he's ready to go knock on his wife's door.

She answers and is not what I expect at all. I want to stand outside and let South go in to find either the warm compress of family or the cold shoulder of blame. Inside of us all are little wars. South is on the top step of his stoop and I am three steps down, on the sidewalk of the street, which makes me feel somehow a part of the landscape, separate from the focus of the scene. Her home is made of bright red brick and is only differentiated by the off-red of her neighbor's home to the right and the grey-painted brick façade of her neighbor's home to the left. The entire block is one long row of houses, separated by interior walls and different colored bricks of mock distinguishability, and from my vantage, it looks like a giant warehouse. I immediately wonder what would happen if one of them caught fire.

South's wife stands at the door and I am surprised at how she looks. I don't know what I expected; perhaps I pictured her as South himself but with longer hair. I don't know; it's strange the way my mind supposes things. In reality, she is small and thin, blond but naturally, and looks very young. She wears no makeup but the contours of her face create shadows in the morning light that shade her face in dynamic contrasts. She is wearing a loose floral print dress with a red belt hugging it to her waist, which produces a feminine form at her center, where it is not evident she has had two of South's children. Standing just outside of her glass door, South seems so much larger than her, rougher. She stands there across from him delicate and docile. South's wife is beautiful and I cannot stop looking at her. Old men have the fortune of perceived generalized dementia; we can stare with innocuousness. I am enamored at the beautiful woman South married.

"Lombard," she says, sonorous. In the one word, a universe of history made frustrated by the happenstance of happenings. Laced within the syllables are simultaneous fear and hope: the *Lom* resonant low and scared with the vendetta that was his popping pistol; the *Bard* caught choking in gladness that he is there. Her saying his name is an entire novel of intricate love and complication. It is a textbook on the anatomy of mankind, and South exhales because it demands his breath from him.

I want to stay outside and guess how far the long rowhomes go, but South introduces me by name and I am up three steps and into his old world before I know it.

In the foyer, she reaches out a tiny hand and says, "Hello, I'm Sidney." Sidney South, a parable in person form. I take it and shake it. We smile at each other and I am so happy for South that it doesn't occur to me that they are divorced, that what has happened to him has happened to him. And as I am a fool, I hope with anything I am deserved, if anything at all, that they can reunite.

I sit on the couch and in the kitchen whistles the warm water Sidney boils for my tea. South and she speak softly in the kitchen and I look at the mantle, where pictures of South still remain. He smiles in them; I've seen him smile before, but this is different. This is the smile of family. He is pictured often with two children, a little blond boy and a little blond girl, with alternating missing teeth in various photographs of development. It feels like how I'd expect it to feel, this fragile little family. Almost immediately, I hear the whispers of the Souths and the screaming water and remember that through their circumstances, those pictured smiles have recessed deep into their faces.

South comes in with the cup of tea for me and is followed by Sidney, who sits next to me on the couch while South sits alone on the one-man plush chair. He leans back in it and breaths in heavily, reminiscent.

"My children are still sleeping," South says, as if answering a question I hadn't posed but that I must have been thinking.

"I see."

"Can we stay until they wake up?" South asks Sidney.

"You can stay as long as you like," she replies. There is no animosity in her voice. I presume that if South wanted to stay permanently, I would be taking a train home. I hope I'll be taking a train home.

She turns to me, "So how did you meet Lombard?"

"We live in the same building."

"Oh, I see. And is this your first time in Philly?"

I nod yes. I'm shy with her, which is frustrating. I'm a boy in school.

"We've been on a road trip sort of, yeah, Old Man?" South says.

"Yes."

"Really?" Sidney says. "You two on a trip? Where have you gone?"

South tells her and I don't think she believes him at first, but she turns to me and I nod again, confirming it. Coming from an old man, it just can't be a lie.

"California?" she says, her disbelief waning but her shock surfacing.

"Yeah," South says. "Clear out to California, and up and back." South pulls out the digital camera he had in his pocket and tells her to scroll through the pictures, to see the state signs proving travel.

"But why?" Sidney asks.

"Why?"

"Well, yeah. Why did you go out to California? Lombard, you didn't tell me you were going to do this."

"It's been a long time, Sid. I didn't know you'd want me to, yeah? To tell you."

"I'm not saying that you had to; it's just strange is all. People don't usually just go to California."

"No," South says, "they don't. Maybe that's why we went."

"You look happy in the pictures," she says. She gets to the one of South on the metal rigging over the highway and says "Christ, Lombard." But it's true, he does look happy in the pictures.

Back in New Mexico, all the way back in New Mexico, at the bar where Bert and Marjorie swiveled their heads in buzzard circles to the tune of their American drinks and American counterparts with their American traumas; South finished the story.

He told me what happened when he found the kid who had killed the cop.

He had become fanatic, wandering the neighborhood streets at all hours, often failing to come home nights in a row. He approached anyone he'd meet in the dead hours, people thin enough to fall through cracks or people without homes enough to return anywhere. He asked questions, intimidated, offered rewards. All of this without the sanction of the department; South was a vigilante, and the less answers he got from his queries, the more his anger grew. I suppose this is the one thing that separates us: anger. I have only loss.

Eventually, because the mysteries of the world move us—chess pieces—to our fated black and white squares, South found the kid. They met in a muddied, abandoned parking lot where the kid had been hiding out.

At that point of the story, I asked South why he always referred to him as a "kid."

"Seventeen," was all he said.

South explained his invigoration, his adrenaline. His pointed gun, the kid on his knees, facing away, hands behind his head. The boy's sudden twitch, the two gunshots, the point-blank range, the slumped figure, the entry wounds at the back, the puddling in front. The stillness.

That night, Bert and Marjorie there but long gone, South told me about the trial. Manslaughter. The city divided: to the cops, the wealthy, the gentrifiers: hero; to the blacks, the impoverished, the imperialized: murderer. Acquittal. Removal. Full pension. The stillness.

He told me of the subsequent disconnect with Sidney and his children. He told me of the entry wounds, the puddling in front, how the kid's chest still heaved involuntary for breath. He told of the instantaneous loss of invigoration, of adrenaline, and of the wild inward rush of shame. South played up the hero card, testified in his own defense about the sudden twitch, the murder of the cop. The kid's rap sheet, arm's length. He went home. The FOP very quietly threw him a "retirement" party; the entire force was in

attendance. The widow of the murdered cop was there, too.
But South sat as alone as he could be with everyone there
coming up to him for handshakes and fond farewells, and
he drank beer. In so many ways, South was gone. His cap-
tain brought up defensive driving in DC. Sidney said,
"Maybe a little time." He said, "Yeah, yeah?" His kissed
his kids each on the forehead. Two parting shots, wet entry
wounds from his lips. The stillness. Then he was on a train
to DC. For that, there was no pardon. I had recognized the
trace of scar.

And eventually, chess pieces, he found me and thought
I was a survivor.

The rumble strips vibrate the road and when I look
over at South, he's wide awake. The car drifts because he's
imagining the potential of the world. He looks over at me
and says, "That's what they're there for."

When his children had woken up, they came down the
stairs together, the little boy leading his sister by the hand.
They saw South suddenly, and he didn't make any moves.
He didn't twitch. Every action by every party was calcu-
lated, like animals hunting in the wild. We were all so very
careful.

Sidney got up and went to the banister of the stairs,
where the children had paused their descent.

"Daddy's here," she said. "Do you want to say hello to
him?"

The boy did not move but the little girl bobbed her
morning messed-up locks with the nodding of her head.

Everyone was cautious, but I sat there feeling separated from a unit that didn't belong to me. Sidney and I
were still on the couch and South was still on the seat, but
he had his two children on his lap and he looked to be torn
between holding them too tightly and letting them play
while simply sitting. He spoke with them and they responded and no one asked the difficult questions: where he

went, why he shot that boy. It was a retreat into pure emotion that people dream of having with others. Calm, safe, and pleasant family love that ignored the fact that this family was still separated. For that moment, they weren't.

We left soon after because the children had school and we needed to get back to D.C. It was a long trip and I feared that I was becoming frightening in the way my beard was so unruly. This was evident in South's children not coming near me. I had wished I would be taking the train home, that South would stay with Sidney and his children, but I knew that it couldn't be, at least not yet. All perfect moments are bracketed with a closed parenthesis that calls an end to the moment and for a resumption of the real world. The real world; how abstract the real world is, especially in its suggestion that moments outside of it are abstractions. Because South knew what it felt like to pull a trigger and have the other end shout the moment he became less human. He was protected by power, by privilege, and lived longer than his victim. He lived, but had survived nothing.

Another rumble and South looks over at me, "It's what they're there for."

Chapter 22

What Mirko thought strange was that no other Permanents were there. This was the sort of parade that the guards and Commander used giddily as a method of instruction. Example by fear. It must have been so truly close to the end, then. The Permanents were old dogs; it was senseless trying to teach them new tricks. Rather, there, were all the guards of camp, standing, encircling. All from the watchtowers, all off-duties and on, high and low ranks, there.

It was February 13, 1945.

Mirko took note of the date. He had not slept since his conference with the Commander. Rather, he was detained in the infirmary while waiting for the sun to rise. He sat on one of the cots and considered sleep, but the glint of the bullet was too bright. The one guard whose task it was to watch him slept on a metal chair that he had leaned on its hind legs against the wall. His head was drawn back and his mouth was open, the choking rasp of apnea galloping steed-like from his plugged throat. The guard's machine gun lay gently across his lap. From Mirko's vantage, he could see out of the small window, and there, to his surprise, was a deer ignorantly grazing on the grass, unaware of the brick buildings that contained thousands of people. Everything was still and the loudspeakers were silent, so the deer did not feel any fear standing in the middle of the camp. Mirko wondered at it, wondered how it was able to get inside, through the electrified wires. Surely there wasn't a gap wide enough for a deer to squeeze through. The thought was somewhat hopeful for him, not that he himself would find the hole and exit by it, but that such a hole existed. That there was proof nothing was impenetrable.

It was a young buck, with the sprouts of antlers on its head just jutting forth and still covered with soft fur. There were white spots on its hind, adjacent to its tail, and the buck walked slowly, deeper into the camp, still unaware that there was anything living inside. Perhaps there wasn't. Perhaps that was why the deer wasn't frightened, Mirko thought, because it knew, surely, that nothing was alive. Only the deer, with its budding antlers and calm gait, was permanent in the temporary place.

Mirko wanted to know the date of his death. He didn't know why, but he wanted to know it, so when the first of the sun shone at the horizon, Mirko turned to the sleeping guard and said, "You."

The guard startled from sleep and, slipping, flung both hands behind him, crashing them against the wall to prevent the chair from falling backwards.

"You are awake," the guard said, oblivious. He was in the world caught between the dreaming and the waking, where neither had enough license on reality to be true. Of course, each second that went by drowned the dream and added to his alertness. He continued, "Yes. You are awake, traitor."

"Traitor?" Mirko asked.

"Yes." The guard held his gun but not by the trigger. He held it like a child, like a cat, across his lap with one hand under for support and the other petting it from the top. Mirko was far enough away that he posed no direct threat. He could see that the guard was young, younger than him. He had never met the guard before.

"How long have you been here?"

"I don't speak to traitors."

"You are speaking to me," Mirko said.

The guard, caught in the paradox, said nothing. Mirko continued, "Why do you call me a traitor?"

At first, the guard paused, but he changed his mind and spoke, "Because you do not serve Germany." His voice was filled with the ignorant enthusiasm of youth and Mirko drank it warmly, remembering.

"My friend, I have served Germany for a long time."

"I know what you have done."

"Tell me, then. Please."

"You aided the prisoners."

"Permanents," Mirko said.

"What?"

"Permanents. That's what we call them."

"That's foolish."

"I think so too."

"I don't care anyway," the guard said; in his wakefulness, he was becoming more alert. It occurred to him that he was still guarding a prisoner, that despite his German soldier's status, this prisoner was just as important, if not more, to guard seriously. "Now stop talking, you are a traitor to your country."

"If I am a traitor to my country than I am a traitor to my countrymen, yes?"

"I said to stop talking."

"And I will. But first, answer my question."

"I will shoot you."

"You will do no such thing. The Commander has bigger plans for me, and it would be very bad for you to spoil them. I could walk over and slap you in the face right now and all you would do is turn red and cry. I could walk right out of here." Mirko exemplified his point by standing up and facing the young soldier. The soldier did not stand, but gripped his gun a little more tightly, enough to make the baby cry. "You see," Mirko said and sat back down. "Answer my question."

"I don't remember it."

"If I am a traitor to my country than I am a traitor to my countrymen. Is that correct?"

"Yes."

"Who are those men in there? In the bunkers?"

"What?"

"Who are they, in there? Your prisoners?"

"They are enemies of Germany."

"Though some are Germans themselves?"

"What?"

"Those men, some, are Germans as well. Isn't that correct? I aided *them*. I aided my countrymen. In what way am I a traitor to this country if I am a brother to its sons?"

The soldier sat silently. He had not thought of this, but more so, did not want to think about it. He was charged with watching a traitor to the country, regardless of what that traitor said. The young soldier was new to the war, barely out of childhood, and one thing that he understood was that he understood none of it. And when that is the case, he surmised, one must do as he is told. He isn't stupid, Mirko thought; he gauged this by his fear. Only a stupid person would be unafraid in this. Still, he would do as he was told, as he should. As he himself had done for years. Registered upon the youth's face was stock confusion, the same facial mannerism of every man caught in a conundrum. There was a neutral face, forced neutral, to not give away the vacuous resolve, with the obvious tear-glossed stare from unblinking and unseeing eyes.

"How long have you been here?"

The soldier again leaned back against the wall. He was more comfortable in that Mirko didn't seem to want to get up and leave, as he threatened. "Three days only. This morning is the start of my third."

"Three days," Mirko reflected. "You will not be here much longer."

"Why?"

"It ends soon."

"The war?"

"All of it. It ends soon. My end and yours. This camp and everyone in it. One way or another, it ends soon. Count yourself lucky."

Mirko looked back to the window and through the panes. The deer had gone. Something must have startled it. Mirko wondered if it knew where to find the aberration in the fence that it entered through. He wondered if it went out the same way. Perhaps it was the buzz of the wires that the deer could hear and knew not to touch. At any rate, it was gone.

"What day is today?" Mirko asked.

"I don't know," the soldier said.

"It is February."

"Yes. It is February. It is the thirteenth, I think."

"Do you know it, or think it only?"

"I arrived on the eleventh. That is a date I will never forget."

"And this one I will remember, at least for what I will know of it, which will not be long. February thirteenth."

"Do you know what they will do?"

"February thirteenth," Mirko repeated, pensively. "They will kill me, for being a traitor." Outside of the window was the same grass of the camp, strangely vibrant with green and vivisected with brown mud streaks where the ground was upturned by passing vehicles. Mirko could hear the static of the loudspeaker cackling to wakefulness, about to deliver the message that all guards should meet by the entrance of the camp, watchtowers and all. The red brick of the bunkers' chimneys contrasted the green of the grass, making a beauty of color. It had rained overnight, so lightly that it was imperceptible; Mirko hadn't heard it against the roof. It was evident only in how brightly the grass showed green against the red chimneys. It was beautiful, as plain as Mirko could figure it. "For being a brother to the sons of Germany," he said.

The other soldiers stood cautiously; they didn't like that Mirko had a loaded pistol. Not one of them thought he was foolish enough to fire it at them—he had only one bullet, after all— but they were uneasy anyway. They stood in a semi-circle with the circus at the center. Mirko and the Kapo. The former with one bullet and one gun, the latter on his knees.

The Commander was there too, with his hair still unruly, standing just on the inside of the semi-circle of guards, watching. There was no extra instruction, no prompt nor lesson for what Mirko had to do, what he had to choose. The bullet was to pass through one human head, and that was all. Mirko's only role was to be the operative to carry out the action. He would point, and he would shoot. He held the pistol at his side, pointed down to the ground, and contemplated firing just like that. It would be a symbol, a suggestion, to shoot nothing but the ground. To shoot the camp itself. But he couldn't. The pistol seemed impossibly heavy in his hand and he was afraid. It was the spectacle, the executioner's block and the salivation of the dogs gathered around him that ripped through his heart with dread. He was filled with treacherous fear, and for it, Mirko was ashamed. He wanted to stand proud at the gallows, swallow, and allow the noose to be knotted at his neck. To put the pistol to his own head, and squeeze as his last act. In the dawn hours in the infirmary, with the young guard leaning against the wall, he felt confident that this is what he'd do, step sturdily on the loose trap door, say his prayer, and swing for his friend. But now, on parade, on stage, the pistol was heavy, and the audience was brutal for the third tragic act. Mirko was angry at his own cowardice. He felt he could no longer stand, but he stood. And next to him, on his knees, facing away, was the Kapo.

Mirko looked down at the Kapo and saw the cowlick spiraling in its renegade tuft on the top of his head. He was in his grey blazer, much too large for him. The blazer hung from the Kapo's shoulders and the bottom of it went straight to the ground; it covered his knees and feet so that it looked like the Kapo didn't have legs at all. He was head and torso, half a man; the soldiers, to a man, thought the image appropriate.

The sky rumbled like a hungry stomach. The rain from the night before was not yet done with its descent and, as all the players and audience looked on, it began to fall with violence. It was a stinging rain, dropping with velocity so that the impact of drops exploded with the thud of a jabbed finger on whatever surface they hit. It was sudden, and it suddenly reminded Mirko of his first day at the camp, with the dogs and the furniture truck and the little boy the Commander helped lift into the box. The coffin. Mirko shut his eyes against the rain and against the memory. There was no way that people could be that way, he thought. No way. His memory forced him to hear the rapping on the sides of the truck, fists vainly forceful, urging to be relieved as the exhaust choked their masters. No way. The dogs and popping of gunfire into the night, bullets meeting the bodies of women, whose filed fingernails were their last hope. No way. The routine intake of Permanents who were led to seemingly endlessly vacant bunks. To showers. No way.

The rain, the pistol, the grey blazer, the mud, the blood, the knees, the bullet.

No way.

This could not be the way of the world.

He opened his eyes to blurred vision. The rain had made mud puddles of the ground around him, a moat separating Mirko and the Kapo from the guards, and his tears met his already wet cheeks. He did not even know he was crying, save for the blurred vision. His hair was water-logged, pasted down unto his forehead and just over the ridge of his eyes. His breathing was in time with his sobs, which he tried to maintain, for his own honor. He succeeded in that neither the guards nor the Commander could see him sobbing. The Kapo, however, could feel the vibrations because of the proximity, and he knew.

"It is okay," the Kapo yelled, over the rain. He was faced away from Mirko, and his body was small and worn, but his voice carried well behind him to Mirko. "It's okay," he said again. "I understand."

Mirko didn't say anything.

"I said it's okay!" the Kapo said, again, more loudly. Desperate. "If you shoot yourself they will only shoot me next. Please, Mirko, do not make your death the last thing I hear. Please."

No way.

Mirko again said nothing. His memory was pacing, quick and frantic, and he was out, crying openly, pride be damned. He had felt this once before in his life, only once, the same feeling. He was a boy, a messenger boy, in Dresden. He was Mirko the Miracle then, running from one side of town to the other without ever losing his breath. In Neustadt, one otherwise unspectacular day, he had just delivered a message. It was noon, Mirko remembered, standing there with the rain so hard that it softened the ground at his feet and he felt himself sink a centimeter, noon because the bells went twelve. He pocketed the coin he was given and was contemplating where to stop for a piece of fruit when he heard tires whine across pavement and the muted rubber thud. Mirko turned his gaze toward the noise, and there, mere feet from him, was a dog lying on its side, on the road, with its tongue full out of its mouth, flat against the blacktop. The car that struck it had moved on a few meters and stopped, its driver getting out to look behind him at the aftermath of the accident. Mirko could not help but notice that the driver checked the front of his car first. He scoffed at the dog, said, "Now someone will learn the investment of a leash," got in his car, and drove off. There were few people around, and after the initial spectacle of the dog's death, they moved on. Mirko, however, approached the struck dog, with its tongue seemingly too long to have ever fit fully in its mouth, and when he neared, the dog's body spasmed with a broken lunge and spat out a small puddle of thick and deeply red blood from its throat. Mirko stood there, over it, and watched its chest move quickly and painfully. He placed his little hand on the quivering body, expecting to soothe it. Not soothing it. Little whimpers came from the dog and the small red puddle grew. Mirko cried there, watching the dog die, not knowing what to do, and it was the same feeling he had there with the Kapo in the rain.

No way.

"Please," the Kapo said again. "Mirko. It is okay."

From behind Mirko, the Commander said, "Erinnerung." He was tired of waiting and was annoyed with the rain. He wanted it to be over so he could retire back into his office and have another glass. As Mirko had presumed, there was no room for pomp in this regard; the German soldier's way was to be quick. Blunt. Cold.

Mirko turned toward the Kapo and raised the pistol to the back of his head. He was careful that the muzzle of the gun did not touch the Kapo. Even then, he did not want to hurt him or to let him know that he was going through with it. He breathed in and the exhale that followed was staccato, trembling motes that hung in the air like resonant notes of a cacophony. His grip on the pistol tightened.

"Mirko," the Commander yelled. "Wait a moment, yes?"

Mirko loosened his grip but did not turn around to face the Commander.

"Miracle," the Commander continued, "do not be so hasty. Prisoner," the Commander's voice, now addressing the Kapo, was as sonorous as if he were talking to a child, cooing it to placation, "please turn around and face soldier Erinnerung."

No one moved. Mirko held the pistol positioned at the Kapo's cowlick, an unintentional bullseye; the Kapo stayed where he was, focused into the distance; the soldiers all stood in their semi-circle, the drama near too much for them.

"Kapo, I asked you to please turn, on your knees, and face soldier Erinnerung. You would be good to follow orders, as you have proved to do so well before. To be a Kapo is, after all, a privilege won by the most fervent of those who can comprehend even the most abstract of commands."

Perhaps it was muscle memory, because the Commander didn't have anything else to threaten the Kapo with. His life expired shortly any way this scene played out, so it followed no real logic that the Kapo would comply to the order, but he did. He revolved, on his knees, small step by small step, difficult in the viscous mud, to turn around and face Mirko. As he turned, he was faced with the black cavern of the pistol's barrel, pointed at his forehead. Somewhere inside, a single bullet gleamed.

"Thank you," the Commander said. "Erinnerung, you may proceed." Mirko could feel the smile on the Commander's face. No way.

Mirko and the Kapo looked at each other, eye to eye, the rain blinking their eyelids. The Kapo wanted to, but couldn't smile. Two men, outside of history, being smothered by it. Between them passed a tenuous energy, pregnant with so much potential, about to be stripped to its barest form: emptiness. On the inside of every man are wonder and defeat. Balanced beauty and scarred ruin. All of this, in a moment, passed between Mirko and the Kapo.

They did not touch, but they were perfectly together for that brief instant.

The Kapo said, "I am Moise." His name. Only and finally. The pistol remained pointed at his face, but he looked passed it, to his friend.

Mirko thought of the beauty of Dresden. Of the Semper Oper. Zwinger. Augustusbrüke. Hofkirche. He imagined himself running around the Frauenkirche, his feet leaping from cobble to cobble, without any knowledge of the grandeur of the world, and all the better for it. In that distant false reality, buried in the most inaccessible store of Mirko's mind, Gregor was still alive. They circled the Frauenkirche together, the huge stones fast together. And Mirko fired.

In Dresden, the ground below the Frauenkirche rumbled, and the stones it was made of burned.

Obligatorily Conciliatory

Chapter 23

My apartment seems much smaller now that I have been out of it for so long. It has been just over a month since South and I drove from here around the country, looking for memories, grounding our lives with glimpses of the past like lightning rods attracting so much energy. I am back at my apartment, but it does not feel like home. The walls have moved closer together, the ceilings dropped. The open space of this great country boxed and confined into my little rooms, ornamented with benign relics of me, holding me against the motion of the world.

When South and I exited the car after the short drive from Philadelphia, we entered our building and a strange moment passed between us. We stood in the foyer, with the metal doors of the mailboxes rowed like the brick homes of South's neighborhood, the single light illuminating the hallways in a strange off-beige color that was unfaithful to the otherwise vibrancy of the colors that made us up. The stairs that led up one floor to South's apartment and two floors to mine were covered in carpet and at the bottom stair, the carpet had pulled up its nails and hung loosely, all skin and no bones, folded upon itself. South and I stood there for a second, knowing that he would stop at one landing and I would proceed on to another. We would part, and for the first time in over a month, we would be alone. He kicked at the flap of carpet and a small cloud of dust released, the particles clinging to light as they descended back to the ground. It was as if we were seeing all that was not usually seen. We breathed in the dust particles but did not feel them in our lungs.

At South's door, he turned and said, "Good one, yeah? The trip and all. Good to get out of here." His sentence was laced with the uncertainty of how to end a long journey. I recognized his uncertainty in my own.

"Yes," I said. "Very good."

"Alright then," he said, "I'll probably come bother you tomorrow. Get some rest."

He paused, because neither of us knew what to do. We simply stood there, looking at one another, everything we couldn't say, said anyway in the silence. South reached up and put his hand against my cheek. He cupped it there only for a second and patted his palm against the white wires of my beard before turning and unlocking his door. When he entered, he turned once more and said, "Get some rest," again.

I suppose he felt it too, the exhaustion of travel. I was more tired than I knew. I went up one more flight of stairs, slower—I was older—and collapsed on my bed for sleep.

Lying in my bed, my arms do not move when I tell them to. They agree, but only after stern petition. I look at the ceiling that has shrunk with the walls and think, if I stay here, it will crush me. But I have no choice; I will stay here. This will be the place I die. For South, he will move back home with his wife and children. At least I hope that's what he'll do. He may not deserve that. But so much happens beyond what one merits. And no one, finally, holds the jurisdictions of fault and forgiveness. I never told him my story. That is what makes the ceiling feel so much closer. And I never will. South will come up to my apartment tomorrow and it will seem like nothing has changed. He will bring a six-pack of beer and we will sit by candlelight discussing every nothing there is to discuss, but I will not tell him my story. My cowardice lies in bed next to me; it will also be crushed by the closing walls.

Now that I am awake, I am realizing that being alone is not as terrible as I feared it would be in the foyer to our building. It has come back so quickly, the loneliness, as if I hadn't traveled with a companion for so long at all. I could have just awoken from a very deep sleep. There could be no Lombard South except for what my brain has imagined a friend to be. What's true is I may have never even left this bed.

A block away, a cock crows at the Vietnamese butchery, so I know I've slept through to early morning.

I pull my left arm out from under the blanket and examine the numbers. They are grey and permanent, always there. The skin above them is raw and calloused from my rubbing, but they are there still, sunk and reminding. There will never be anything I can do to remove these numbers from my forearm. They are a part of me, distorted digits that are not mine, but that saved my life.

I can remember South only calling me by my actual name once. Traditionally, the snarky *Old Man* epithet was his branding for me, the hot cattle brand more what I am than who I am. Old. A Man. Burned into my skin, another keepsake unasked for. Though, in this case, I am not offended by what South calls me, as I know it is a term of endearment. I gladly wear the namesake: *Old Man*; after all, the pseudonym is not a misnomer.

It was spoken to Sidney, his wife. When I entered, he said, "Sid, this is my friend. Mirko Erinnerung." She contemplated repeating it to understand if she had heard right, but she didn't dare to try. That beautiful woman, she had the presence of mind to not be rude, even though I know my name must have sounded very foreign to her.

She welcomed me, and I said, "Miracle."

"Pardon me?" she said.

"Mirko. My name. It sounds like the English word for Miracle."

CHAPTER 24

It was said that the enemy was one day out of camp and advancing. Word from Berlin, quiet word, was that the war was indeed ending, and that Germany would again be held at the mercy of the rest of the world. It would take up its penitent cross from Europe. Approaching, a day away, was an army of machines and young men, unaware of the grounds upon which they were about to happen. This is what the Commander thought as he contemplated his orders. For a long time, perhaps forever, they would not know what they were walking into. A field of chimneys, where the wooden bunkers they once serviced no longer stood; the remains of brick buildings whose twisted metal insides were little more than wartime curiosities, left over for the misinterpreted presumptions of historians. A railroad track ending nowhere. Fences marking the perimeter of nothing. The approaching army would never know. And years from now, the Commander thought to himself, rubbing the paper between his thumb and forefinger, on which his orders were written, when the historians come, they will attempt to piece together the strange workings of the camp and make a critical, ethical condemnation that would serve as the low-water mark for morality. He looked down at the paper with disdain, the sinews of his arm tempted to crumble. What good were orders from a dying city anyway? You could not be a traitor to the cooling coal of a spent inferno. He would prefer to leave the camp intact, to allow the approaching soldiers to see how it actually was, in its glory and its squalor. They should see the Permanents and their hollow eyes gazing out forever untrustingly, the brick buildings engineered perfectly for their purpose, the strict operating standards that were at the pinnacle of functionality, the apex of human success, at least in terms of in the completion of its goals. You cannot blame a machine for its program.

His brow was scrunched upon itself as he stared down into the message. *Destroy the camp*, it said, only. To himself, he questioned it. Why? Now, at the admission of our defeat, are we so contrite that we attempt to align with the moral perception of the rest of the world? There was something about destroying the camp that the Commander thought was ulterior to the purpose of it being built. If Germany was to be judged for the camp and its workings, then so be it. Defeated in war, yes, but in our national consciousness, we should not conform to our successful enemy. I have spent too many years of my life in this, the Commander thought, to admit that it was wrong enough to shame and destroy. If there was shame in its building, it should not have been built. And now, with the enemy approaching, we are to deliver from it any consciousness of our guilt. What subtle cowardice.

The whiskey had been exhausted for quite some time and its absence made him righteous. He sat alone in his office with the message gripped in both hands, greased thumbprints smeared into the corners. The soldiers outside were nervously anticipatory, unable to control the small shakings of their bodies; but inside, the Commander's office was as tidy as the day he entered it. His papers were in order in cabinets that lined the wall to his left. In front of him, behind glass and supported by a dark wood frame, was a topographical map of Germany that acted as the backdrop to whomever he was interviewing. He gazed at the map, the bold lines that separated states and even bolder lines that suggested foreign nations. The contour lines that suggested elevation. It was an old map, from the first War, unusable as it no longer represented the furthest boundaries of the country. It was given to him as a gift, at the granting of this position, to remember the Germany that was, and what it could become. When it was first given to him, he studied it, and was bewildered at how drawing new lines on a paper such as that could indicate the nationality of the people who lived within the terrain. Where nationality was so important to mankind, it was as arbitrary as bold lines.

He had the map framed immediately.

Looking at it there, in his office that was soon to be ash, piled grey leaves that disappear in wind and underfoot, he could not help but wonder what aberrations, what slashings of new bold lines would vivisect the country and make foreigners out of neighbors. It was a bad business, cartography, he thought to himself. To be charged with making allegiances out of the positioning of men. He pitied the map-makers more so than he did even himself. At the end of things, both war and peace included, the one commonality that proved true regardless of circumstance, was that there was no recourse but to accept change. With the ending of each movement came the spur to prod another progress.

He got up from his desk and walked around to the door. Exiting, the soldiers on guard looked at him and he spoke directly, with as much authority as he usually commanded, "Down, the camp shall burn."

Mirko's knees hurt somewhere inside. The legs, which had thrust him with such wild haste around the streets of archaically vibrant Dresden so many years before, had begun to swell so that bending them would provoke a tightness that hurt and confused him. The swollen, locking hinges of his legs, the propellants of his youth, were now protesting their own function, as if aware of a new and great spiritual dearth upon the man they helped to stand.

Mirko was unavailable to everyone. The Commander was satisfied with the spectacle of the Kapo and did not speak again, neither out of warning nor reconciliation, to his soldier. Rather, Mirko was left to continue his duties at the camp, which he did, out of simple apathetic muscle memory. He did his duty because it was programmed of him. Otherwise, he was drained of everything that propelled the child who carried messages to the businessmen of Dresden. The child who, walking over Augustusbrüke, encountered the endlessness that was the rest of life. The child who was alive amidst an environment of old things.

Mirko was a man whose body was vacated. The flighty would call it spirit, the religious: soul; but whatever Mirko was before his right hand squeezed that day in the rain was replaced with a facsimile that could not bring its eyes from the ground. He went about his duties, manning the towers, standing guard, but always, his eyes were lowered to the ground.

His knees were swollen, almost to the point that he had to walk without bending them. He was a spectacle on stilts, alternating a tottering step, but no one laughed. Even the lunacy of the swollen-kneed soldier's gait wasn't enough to liven even a moment of the expected end.

When the orders came for him to do his part to destroy the camp, his eyes did not rise in surprise and fear, as the rest of the soldiers' did. He did not question the command and turn his poor head to the side to ask if he had heard right. Unlike the other soldiers, Mirko did not stall and stutter a shocked response. He took the three grenades he was proffered and walked slowly toward the incinerator, as was his charge.

Berlin was wrong; the enemy was not a day away. From the distance, the long lines of Allied troops heard the slow drone of big explosions and advance scouts returned to inform the company that, only a few miles away, was a German civilian camp, presided upon by outnumbered and under-gunned soldiers. They were setting fire to the camp's bunkers and blowing up its brick buildings.

As Mirko walked toward the building he was to destroy, the Allied troops had mobilized and were already approaching, anticipatory with their sure capture.

The Permanents stood huddled together in the most open part of the camp while the soldiers set fire to the bunkers. They were confused, and nothing of the panic in the eyes of their captors provided them with any comfort. The heat from the burning buildings, which used to be their homes, provided them with comfort. As their shelters burned, and with it, the remnants of their lives, the heat thawed their stiff bodies, energy both created and destroyed. Some felt strangely nostalgic for the burning buildings. They were prisoners there, suffering atrocities beyond articulation, but within the bunkers were the beds they slept in nightly, which, even if illusion, were still home. By the time Mirko reached the door of the brick building that housed the incinerator, fires had been set to the majority of bunkers and already two buildings were now the scatterings of brick. The smoke from the burning buildings traveled both up and out, so it was difficult to breathe. He entered and, locating the incinerator, placed the three grenades in the center. He rigged the three pins with a metal wire, which would allow him to pull all of them simultaneously, and tested the tautness of the line. It was firm; when he tugged carefully, all three pins budged a millimeter, and he let the wire go.

Outside, he could hear the shouts of the other soldiers to hurry. Their own scouts had come back and, breathlessly, told the Commander that the Allied company was great and approaching, and would be there within two hours. The Commander instructed his men to destroy the camp at twice the speed and began to prepare a convoy of trucks for them to leave, as soon as the last building was gone. Despite everything, the Commander was a rational man. This characteristic was what won him his position.

He had always been able to see, with great foresight, what
was coming. When the scouts returned, he knew very well
that there was little to no chance his soldiers would be able
to evacuate and completely destroy the camp. It, then, became a choice. Berlin had wanted the camp destroyed. It
was the destruction of the camp or the lives of his men. The
day was as clear, bright, and beautiful as he could remember, but the smoke made the sky overcast and nefarious.
He had to choose soon.

"And of the Permanents?" asked one of his direct subordinates.

"We leave them here," he said.

"Do we shoot them?"

"We save the bullets for ourselves."

Mirko paused at his work and briefly exited the building. He had never been to the front of a battle but this was
how he pictured it to be. Smoke rose in Romanesque pillars
in all directions and seemed to hold up the sky. He felt like
he was in a great temple, moving and organic, as the smoke
pillars swelled like muscles and rose. The smell of burning
was dominant and intrusive, but it did not smell like one
thing; it was a great many things, perhaps everything, becoming ash. Mirko watched the ash, snowing from the
black towers as if a flock of overhead birds was letting loose
its feathers. It coated everything in a momentary grey-
white then melted with the subtlest gesture. As the ash of
the camp swirled at each gust of wind, Mirko thought that
it was the end of the world, and that the end, in all its ter-
ror, was part beautiful. He inhaled and a flake of the ash
entered his nose. When it reached his throat, he coughed,
and wondered for a second what real thing he had consumed after it burned and became a grey remnant. It could
have been a bunker or a body. Either way, it was in him.
He turned and went back into the building.

Inside, Mirko reached down and placed his left hand on the three grenades while with his right, he pulled the metal wire connected to their three pins. He had a total of six seconds before the grenades would blow after he released them and the handles dropped away. Even then, after everything, he still had enough instinct for survival that he prepared himself to rush while counting the six seconds.

Mirko lifted his hand and the three handles separated from the grenades, arming them. He turned and started to move quickly toward the door, his knees so swollen that his legs were locked straight. It was difficult for him to be agile and fast, but the door was only a few strides away, and he made the entrance with four seconds to spare. He swung his left leg, at the hip, over the small step that rose from the ground to meet the door, and was pulling the other through when it caught the step, hooking at the toe, and dragging him to the ground. As the majority of his body pitched forward into the Armageddon of the world outside, he heard the distinct click of the mechanisms activating behind and felt an incredible rush of warm wind enveloping him, throwing him, with broken stone and blackened metal, into the torrents of the abyss.

A blossomed flower of inverted steel was left. The bricks closest to the ground, sometimes stacked up to six high, were undisturbed, as if the blast rose and caught only the highest part of the structure. The lower bricks, still in their places, looked like the floor plan of the building, the perimeter wall suggesting where a building should be, though no building was. Inside the perimeter bloomed the skeleton of a steel square, bent at the center of each of its bars, so that the sides seemed to move out, caught or paused in a midair dance of separation. It was not possible, at first glance, to discern what the structure was. All that could be surmised was that the components of the steel structure were stuck moving away from one another.

In the absence of the German soldiers, the camp was disturbingly quiet. For the Permanents, who had lived under the assault of the loudspeakers and had to respond to the enraged commands of the guards, and who were threatened by the ferocious barks of the dogs, the silence was unsettling. A great many of them remained huddled around the burning bunkers, to stay warm and to hear the cracking of the wood as if it were violating the silence. Others, the stronger, younger, and most recent to the camp, went off exploring, looking for remnants of food and supplies.

When the soldiers left, they locked the fence behind them, and the Permanents had not yet the desire to risk the fence's electric potential. They felt safer now in the camp than outside of it, where it was unknown just how far the nearest sanctuary would be and where the cold terrain was uninviting.

The Commander had made his choice; he was impatient with how long the dismantling process was taking, and feeling his allegiance to Berlin crumble with the caving bunkers and that unsatisfactory note, he executed a full evacuation of his men. He set fire to his office and for a moment, imagined the old lines of the world burning away, before turning and issuing the order. They took only what was on their persons, boarded trucks, locked the gates, and began driving away from the camp, which was left only half-destroyed. He did not bother counting his men or checking to see who was left behind. In truth, he knew that he wouldn't get far even with the evacuation. It was only a matter of time before the approaching army caught up with them. One way or another, they would be caught, and perhaps reunited with the men they had left.

He drove at the front of the motorcade, facing out of the front window, and did not look into the side mirrors to see the camp burn. He faced forward, to the open road, and did not think of the Permanents huddled together in the center of the camp, skeletons abandoned. He did not think of his own fate, about what the enemy would do to him when they caught up with him. He did not imagine a firing squad or a noose to his neck. He thought only of Germany. The scars that now marred its complexion. Youthful knife fights. He thought of it as a field of snow after the year's first snowfall, unblemished and completely level, equal in the white plainness that covered everything uniformly underneath. Then he pictured footsteps and motorcars traveling over the field, disturbing the white unity of the ground, turning the field into a sodden and filthy grey.

Out the windshield, the road turned around a pass, obscuring the next.

Mirko awoke to a close subtlety; the camp was quiet beyond the wood coal's seething and from his vantage point on the ground, there was a stillness not even dared tread upon by the wind. He was prostrate, as still as the nearby grass, and could not tell if it was in his ability to move. He sampled a toe, lifting it to curl, and then tried another. Obeying his command, he allowed the toes to slump as his chest also did, upon the Earth. It may have been an illusion, it may have been a fiction his mind demanded, but a certain heaviness kept at his back, heaped and mired between his shoulder blades to pin him—dead butterfly—to the camp ground. He breathed and the force of it twittered the blades of grass nearest his mouth. He stared at the blur of everything around him. Nothing held a sharp focus; the edges of things, once so corporeal in their boundaries, dissipated at their fringes to allow the substance of each thing to squeeze through. Reality itself was porous. It detained neither thing nor concept, but left wide open—like a gaping pit, like an anarchic cauldron of crisping bodies— the heart from a chest. No more was humanity vulnerable against itself; it had traveled beyond the turbulence of vulnerability into a terrain from which it could never return: a scarred insides where, from then on, when one looked into the eye of another, there could be seen a corruption so complete that it consumed the body like a cancer, but a cancer so large it was impossible to know when the body stopped and the disease began.

Nothing held a sharp focus, not even Mirko. There was no division between the boy he had been and the soldier he was. Any hope of redemption in the acknowledgement that he had been a boy and that that boy was stripped to bareness by the great mechanisms of the world was moot in the substance of the camp. The *thatness* of the camp being the camp. It provided no answers and allowed for no rationalization. There was as much *not* Mirko as there was Mirko. It had swallowed him only because he had swallowed it; and in the impossibility of the ouroboros, the final consequence was that all reduced to nothing. The grey ash of all things burned out to leave feathered oblivion too delicate even for the wind.

And then he saw it. A deer. Perhaps *the* deer. Walking slowly, head held regal, away from him. Everything was soot-covered except that deer's flank, its footsteps leaving ash prints in negative on the landscape. Its gait was so sure that Mirko convinced himself of the deer's complete ignorance of all that was around him. For that, Mirko felt the final sting of envy. It moved away from him, its budding antlers points against a sky sodden with all that was burned into it, and kept going until it was forever beyond Mirko's view.

He did not know about the incinerator behind him; he could feel only that the back of his shirt was burned away and that the raw flesh of his back met the air without any resonating sensation, pain or otherwise. He did not care to move, did not care to ever again try his muscles against gravity. He wanted, instead, to sink, to allow the weight to keep upon his back until it pushed him through the surface of the ground and did not stop until his heart did. Why, he wondered, was he spared from the explosion? At this, this end of it all, how was it possible he could still be there? What mystical treachery demanded him to live on?

Without being able to identify the direction of the sound, he heard voices. Two Permanents, nearby, speaking.

"You were a student?" one asked.

"I *am* a student."

"Ah, yes. A lost book is still a book," the first said. "A man, the same. And those eyes of yours."

"I know."

"And your hair."

"Yes."

"You could have passed."

"Easily."

"And why did you not?"

"I could have walked among them."

"Tell me."

"Because then I would not be the book."

The men moved on, either not taking notice of Mirko or, having seen so many bodies, presumed him to be just another. He feared them, feared their retribution as the man who deserves it vainly struggles to claim he should be spared. When they were gone, Mirko thought more keenly of his actual impending fate. He knew the enemy army was approaching and when they arrived, there would be little more to do than follow the course of the rest of his life. He would be upon rails that would end somewhere.

Then something made a muscle twitch. It was against his will, but it proceeded to wave from one sinew to the next, an animal demand beyond his intention. His brain, without his accord, fired impulses to his extremities and the twitches became tenses, which became the movements of appendages. He tried to rally against them, demanding them to stillness. He near pleaded to stay. Prayed to remain. To die, like man. Like the idea of man. He did not think of Dresden, of Gregor and Adette. He did not remember the transit around cobbled streets, nor of the conversations with Moise. He didn't even think about how he once was a thing and now was another thing, a changed, spoiled thing with no single explanation to ever tranquilize the nothing of all that was left.

What he thought about was the approaching army. His final cowardice.

Mirko slid from under the debris that held him; the weight on his back was more than his life; it was part of the building he'd been tasked to destroy. He discovered that he was whole but was unable to convince his legs to do much more than aid his crawling. The movement out of the rubble brought new pains to him, things he'd never felt. Still, he crawled through the ash to a body some yards away. It was still, spent, a Permanent; dead for an indecipherable amount of time. Their bodies were not substantial enough to distinguish much from corpses, so there was no way to truly know how long ago that man was alive.

Mirko stripped the body of the grey, rough clothing that covered the man, working slowly between struggling breath and the ever-awakening nerves of his afflicted body. The clothing slid away without protest, the man's body having not enough substance to hold purchase on the material. Mirko then began to disrobe himself. His uniform was so decimated from the explosion that it was not difficult to shed. A snake, his old skin discarded in torn clumps next to the naked Permanent, Mirko dressed in the grey.

He looked down at himself, in the costume of his lie, but knew it wasn't enough. His body was too full; it contained too much being. He would need something more, and he knew what more he needed.

Mirko drug himself back toward the incinerator. Its brick walls scattered haphazardly and its iron inside skewed to ugly distortion, the building was difficult to access. At the center, impossibly, was a clay bowl—he did not know how it had gotten there—that was somehow spared from the explosion. It was whole. Pandora's hope. A hoax, he thought. He inched upon his belly around the parts of the machine, careless as to how it tore at his new clothes, disinterested in what it once was. Soon, they would arrive. They would use foreign speech, these men, who came from other places to be there. Who willfully marched toward the camp as if it was any place on Earth. He scoured the ground looking but nothing matched his query.

He heard a commotion nearby but did not bother to understand what it meant. Did he hear the chains of the fences fall apart? Was that the roar of war in the vehicles of the enemy for whom he had no animosity? Did he hear the faint gasp of the chorus of Permanents as they breathed out in the direction of their liberators? He had little time and little consciousness remaining.

Mirko managed to drag himself to the center of the building, to the incinerator's machine core, and searched carefully amongst the contorted innards. It was there he found them. Rudely contorted shards of shrapnel from the incinerator, all deeply blackened with burned soot. He chose the sharpest. Where he held it, the dark soot transferred to his palm.

Mirko rolled his new sleeve to the elbow, aimed the tip of the sooted metal to his forearm, and dug numbers.

CHAPTER 25

They are permanent: sunk, still, and always.

And I've survived nothing.

Blue flame seems unnatural, but it is sufficient in its heat. I hover my hands above, letting the warmth find my fingers, as Moise taught me to. His name rings in my memory, like a struck bell, and though I am careful to not let my hands lower into the stovetop's burner, my memory's loud sounds disturb my concentration, and I again smell burnt human hair. Moise. I hear the one sound, the way it came from his mouth. His tongue and lips, shaping sound, pronouncing his name. I carry that sound more deeply in my skin than the soot and grease scars that saved my life. You get what you pay for but you also pay for what you get. Moise. Always.

He died, because I didn't have the courage to.

It rains outside of my apartment and because of it, the sky above the rooftops is a threatening grey. I hear the sirens of an ambulance and leave the burner to go to the window and look. Its flashing presence creates disarray in the other vehicles on the street; they contort into odd shapes along the shoulders of the road, creep into oncoming traffic, honk at one another to move, gamble out into an intersection: so that the ambulance can weave through. Priority. A culture where the ambulance itself is more revered than the dying. The people walking by with umbrellas create a current of moving domes, all magnificent instances of color gliding down the sidewalks, turning corners and disappearing. They no longer exist. The burner on my stove still roars blue and is the only thing moving in my apartment. The reaching flames seem real and vibrant, and I smell the gas that is their breath, pushing up through the pipes in my floor and igniting. Burning. Seared

knuckle hairs curl into the fetal position, their balled tips
but ash to brush away. The scent lingers. And my fingers
are always bald, regardless of how careful I am.

Moise.

I examine the buildings of Washington D.C through
the racing streaks of rain on my window. They congregate,
densely, in blocks as far as I can see, and I cannot help but
to think of how sturdy they look, how permanent, as if
nothing could ever shake the ground around their founda-
tions. I remember thinking this of the buildings of Dresden
as well. The Frauenkirche, more magnificent than any
building I've ever seen. I understand they are rebuilding
it in Dresden, putting it back together. Perhaps I will see
it. I am more travel-savvy now. Although, I cannot imagine returning to Dresden. It will not be the place I remember. After we returned from our memorial hunt, South
went to the library and took out every book he could find
about the bombing. He said the photos near made him cry.
What he actually said was, "I didn't get it, yeah? What you
meant and all, about it not being there. But then I saw the
pictures, yeah? The pictures they had, Old Man, you
wouldn't believe. It looked. . .it was just. . .nothing. It was
a city of walls, but that's all. No buildings but a wall, here
and there, and..." and he broke off in that obvious way. So
he didn't actually say that they nearly made him cry, but I
could tell.

So I look at the buildings here in D.C. and I know that
they are here now, but they may not always be. That all it
takes is a moment to take something beautiful and make it
nothing. But they are rebuilding the Frauenkirche, from
what I understand. That is good. That means something.
Perhaps one day South will see photos of the reconstruction
and he'll smile. Perhaps, one day, his children will run
around it. If it is ever reconstructed, I suppose I will have
to admit that beauty can bloom again.

Moise.

The name rings like a bell, every hour, on the stroke. *Moise Moise Moise*, when it's three.

What becomes of self-discovery when I do not like what I discover? I watch children and I see how cruel they can be to animals, as if it is innate. I watch the television and see other great towers smolder and collapse, because all of mankind is a truant schoolboy, too lazy to learn from its past mistakes. Over and over, he builds into the sky. Over and over, he collapses what he creates. I see men with torn clothes and their backs against buildings, with their legs over grates that emit great clouds of white steam; they look absently into the crowd as people walk in wide arches around them. Seventeen-year-old boys shoot at police officers, and a detective shoots back. Mothers die and children work in a factory to support their siblings. It is almost too much to consider all at once. I look out the window at the raining world, the grey skies above deepening, and I find it hard to want to be part of this. But I am. And someone once built the Frauenkirche. Someone is rebuilding it.

All of it wrapped together in this world.

"It's unnatural."

"What?"

"The rain. It's unnatural."

"Nothing's unnatural. If it happens, it is natural."

"'Nothing's unnatural.' This guy. It's been raining for a straight week. You'd forget there was a sun."

"But there is."

"Yeah, Old Man, there is. You're right. What's the point? All I'm saying is, wait, anyway, yeah? Forget it."

South takes a quick drink from his beer and looks out the window, shakes his head at the precipitation, the falling water. Nothing could be more natural, but I don't say this to him. I just let him shake, the oscillation of his face reflecting against the light-polluted window. He's been

here a half hour but hasn't taken off his coat. The cold cuts
through the artificial heat and the machinery that pumps
warmth through the vents in my floor is loud as it rumbles
double-time, trying to play victor over the winter.

"Have you spoken with Sidney?" I ask. South's attention is momentarily drawn away from the window. He
looks at me; from where he's sitting, he looks like a contem-
plative academic, wrapping his mind around an abstrac-
tion.

"Yeah," he says. I don't ask anything else. The prose-
cution has no further questions, your honor. All the world's
in that word.

"What's with you?" he asks.

"What?"

"You're drenched. Soaking."

I look down at myself, "So I am."

"Were you playing out there, or do I have to worry you
have dementia?"

"You don't have to worry."

"Good. Because I don't want to."

"I don't want you to."

"Yeah."

He sits in my kitchen chair, looking out into the world.
I watch him, a weak old man, my own skeleton in my closet.
But he is so sincere in his friendship to me. I am not char-
ity to him. I'm simply a person he knows. And he is a person I know. And as close as we'll ever be is as far away as
we are right now.

Before South came over, I went for a walk. I did not
bother to bring an umbrella; the falling rain had pleaded to
hit against my head, I felt invited by it, so I left my apartment and found myself on the sidewalk, waterlogged in moments. After the initial shock of my clothes dampening and

bearing the subtle weight of saturation, it was almost as if I didn't realize it was raining at all.

I made my way to a small park, a grassy triangle of undeveloped real estate created by the intersection of three streets, and sat down on a sodden bench. The grass was bright green in the rain. Car tires dipped into pavement recesses and sent eyelash curved waves into the air; as the independent drops landed, I heard a series of slaps to the tune of their splatters. Those who walked by, with umbrellas overhead, moved a bit more quickly than usual, as if, in haste, they could lessen their exposure to the rain. I wanted to tell them of the wonder of letting the rain just hit them, but didn't know where to start.

A young woman with a rabid Shih Tzu leashed to her wrist struggled with the umbrella in her other hand as the wind tried to claim it. It inverted, and she stabbed at the air to right her sanctuary. A little boy, her son, danced in the sky's waterfall. He was dressed in a slick yellow jacket made from either plastic or vinyl, and he had a wide-brimmed hat to match. I watched him as the rain ran from it off the edge of the brim, making a bee keeper's mask of water around his head. He ambled over to me on my bench in the peculiar trusting way of children who are brave when they are conscious of their mother's presence behind them. I waved to her as she bent down to remove from the ground what the dog had deposited and she smiled at me. A sign of acceptance. The fragile old man on a bench, soaked through, odd but not dangerous. It had taken a long time, but I was glad to not be seen as dangerous anymore. I had shaved.

The boy slapped the bench next to where I was sitting, sending a tiny spray of water into the air. His mother called for him to settle down but he didn't pay her any mind. He looked at me, smiled, and did it again. His hands were smooth. I remember thinking that they could become calloused with work. He smiled at me, then struck the

bench again. I mimicked his action with the feeble pat of
an old man, the veins almost black in my hand, and he gig-
gled. We slapped away at the bench and the rain continued
to refill what we sent flying.

His mother called a final time, this time with a touch
of warning in her voice. The touch inspired his instinct and
he ran off without so much as a goodbye, though I didn't
expect one. One bench: one person just starting life and
one who had come to the end of it. That is how life is; it is
a spectrum with warmth at one end and chill at the other.
There is the beauty of entering it all, and the grotto of
shame that comes from preparing to leave it. In between,
are years of experience that are full of wonder and worry.

I looked after the boy and his mother and wondered
what he'd become. What he'd be forced to become. My gen-
eration has scars all over its face but children are born
without scars. If I had the courage to tell South my story,
he'd find so much sympathy in me that he'd try to convince
me that I did what I had to do. But he'd be wrong. I had
to do nothing. What I did, I did. He would hope it, but for
me, there cannot be redemption.

Moise.

It echoes around the caverns of my mind. It is a permanent memorial, something South couldn't drive me to,
because I am already there.

I think often about my childhood in a place that no
longer exists. I think about the cobbles and of my mother,
whom I never knew apart from the sister who looked like
her. It never made me sad as a child, but it makes me sad
now. It's the awareness that does it. The last vision I had
of Adette's white eyes shines to me at the end of a tunnel
that sinks through the Earth into my past. If she is alive,
I do not know it; but I imagine her, somehow alive in the
hollow of Dresden, reading Bible lines and nodding at the
significance of them. I've absorbed the brunt of history,

this whole and entire human failure, but I make no illusions that I am outside of it. History is made of actions the way societies are made of people. And I am a person who acted. I am a living history of society and I am destined soon to feel a cool white sheet everywhere upon me. It will drop evenly and all at once, and I will know the proximity of the closure. Alone in my apartment, I tremble. South is a floor below, lesson planning for the next Defensive Driving class. I sit in a chair against the wall and lean my head back until it touches. I watch the window. South and Moise and I. Dresden and Gregor and the whole world. Alive before the falling of a cool white sheet. All permanent: sunk, still, and always.

With the morning my alarm will cry, set at six, and the captive cocks, pleading down the block, will wish again for open air.

EPILOGUE

In 1743, a cross was placed on the top of the Frauenkirche in Dresden, Germany, completing a structure that would awe Europe in its grace and weightlessness for centuries. Although a Lutheran Church, the building stood as a symbol of architectural beauty and ingenious engineering for all of Dresden's residents, who could see the great sandstone dome lift above the cobbled streets of the city by the Elbe river, the Florence of the Elbe. The elegance and ornate liveliness of the Frauenkirche's rising cupola, its bright masonry, and the impressive Silbermann organ nestled within the nave of its muraled inner dome impressed travelers who came and were warmed in the cast shadow of its slender but august form, including Wilhelm Robert Wagner, who conducted debuts of his most famous works in the building.

But beyond the obvious national and civic pride the Frauenkirche brought to its admirers and to the land from which it rose, it became a symbol of human art: in that mankind was able to imagine, design, and produce concepts of beauty that interconnected all people who appreciated its walls, regardless of the borders they were born behind, the faiths of their religions, or the conditioned languages of their tongues. Perhaps it was not universally appreciated, as the joys of experience for one are mere trivialities for others, but as a symbol, an object of expression, the Frauenkirche stood to suggest what beauty mankind could make, if it so chose.

In February 1945, mankind also chose, suggesting that as beautiful it can be, mankind can be just as devastating. On an Allied air raid on Dresden, the Frauenkirche sustained critical fire and structural damage from incendiary bombs dropped on the city, destroying almost the entire historic center and leveling the Frauenkirche to a pile of charred-black stone. Only a small wall remained. The wall had a high arching window that peered into nothing, a phantasm remnant of what the city had once been. Many historical texts have been presented both condemning and justifying the attack on Dresden, and I do not mean to offer additional editorial on the subject. Rather, I choose to focus on the loss of the one structure, which was at some point a symbol of beauty, reduced to a reminder of havoc.

Before writing *Permanent for Now*, I spent some time in Dresden, thinking of the city that stood before me, which glowed in the evening while I rested on its Augustusbrüke. My companions had walked on toward our room in Neustadt while I remained behind, saddened and guilt-ridden about my country's part in its destruction while promising its sidewalks in some lofty, romantic way that I would write it beautifully. I did not want to write a book about Nazi Germany, nor about the Holocaust. Nor did I want to write a book about characters who could never be redeemed for the transgressions they committed against their fellow man. South and Mirko are not redeemable characters; the discomfort we feel in them not facing their crimes is meant to mirror the soreness history leaves for us. It is an unsettledness we cannot reject because it is present in the very stones that make us. The architecture of human identity is spotted with such discolored stones, and so too must literature make us yearn for a resolution that cannot come. I, instead, wanted to write a book about the *conundrum that is man*: how we can maintain both goodness and evil within the same spirit. After all, I, too, am a man; so the beauty of those who built the Frauenkirche is in me, as is the depravity of those who built the concentration camps. I needed to rectify this for myself, as a son of Jewish ancestry, and as a writer whose work has always been about exploring what confounds me the most; thus, the book was born.

As I stood on Augustusbrüke, ashamed and saddened,
I looked at the Frauenkirche, finally rebuilt in 2004, gleaming with magnificence where it had stood for centuries before the war, safely by the Elbe. Mathematicians, architects, and historians came together to sift through the rubble, calculate blast radii, and reconstruct (with new materials as well as some of the original stone) what was destroyed. For me, it was again a symbol: that mankind could create, that it could destroy, and that it could create again; that the good of our spirit does not cancel out the evil, but that it rejects it, by building upon the rubble it creates. This became the sole optimism I found in all the sludge and soot of the subject matter. For me, this closed the literary resolution.

The Frauenkirche stands in Dresden.

It should not be taken for granted, as it may not always stand. It may not remain permanent. But it should be celebrated, because for now, it is.

ABOUT THE AUTHOR

Jeffrey S. Markovitz is the author of the novel *Into the Everything* (2011) and the story chapbook *—for Olivia* (2013). His fiction, non-fiction, and poetry have appeared in publications such as *The Cardiff Review*, *The Saint Katherine Review*, *The Swamp Literary Magazine*, *Evansville Review*, *ellipsis*, *Glassworks*, *Kindred Magazine*, *Apiary Magazine*, *Certain Circuits Lit Mag*, *Transient*, *Spittoon*, *Prime Mincer*, *Scribble*, *Origivation*, *Specter*, *Hidden City Philadelphia*, and *Philadelphia Inquirer*. He lives in Philadelphia, where he teaches English.

Catch up with Markovitz at his website:
jeffreysmarkovitz.wordpress.com

ABOUT THE PRESS

Unsolicited Press was founded in 2012 and is currently based in Portland, Oregon. The team works to produce excellent poetry, fiction, and creative nonfiction. Learn more at www.unsolicitedpress.com.